The Writers Afterlife

A NOVEL

Richard Vetere

THREE ROOMS PRESS
NEW YORK

To Lisa

The Writers Afterlife
a novel by Richard Vetere

First Edition

ISBN: 978-0-9884008-8-7
Library of Congress Control Number: 2013947720

Cover and interior design:
KG Design International
katgeorges.com

Three Rooms Press
New York, NY
threeroomspress.com

"I am borne darkly, fearfully, afar;
  Whilst, burning through the inmost veil of Heaven,
  The Soul of Adonais, like a star,
  Beacons from the abode where the Eternal are."

"Adonais: An Elegy on the Death of John Keats"
PERCY BYSSHE SHELLEY

"Ambition is the last refuge of failure."

OSCAR WILDE

CHAPTER 1

I died typing midsentence in a T-shirt and boxer shorts in front of my computer. I was about halfway into the second act of a screenplay. I had taken the job to buy me the time to write the novel I had been thinking about for a year. I also thought the money could sustain me while I tried looking for a producer to bring my latest play into production.

The screenplay I was writing was a job for hire. It wasn't much of a challenge, though I was trying my best to make sense out of the story. It was a typical writing assignment my agent would get me: idiosyncratic characters and quirky dialogue that nearly everyone with Final Draft believed they could mimic just by watching *Goodfellas.*

However, the professionals knew I did it better than the hacks. I lived it, and the sounds of that life resonated in my brain. I had a sincere ear for the music in the dialogue without spoiling it with irony; I tackled each rewrite, each project with a silent passion knowing I was the best.

I wish I'd been working on the novel in my head when I died. I hadn't worked out the details, but wanted it to be about why I had become a writer in a family in which my father and mother hardly spoke to each other. Yes, it was another novel about a dysfunctional family—but that was what was expected of a contemporary novel that hoped to be taken seriously. I wish I'd been working on anything other than that stupid movie. Right before I died, my last thought was, *I wonder who they are going to get to rewrite me.* I was pretty sure it was going to be Warren Fabrizi.

Fabrizi was also represented by my agent, whose name was Claudia Wilson, and he always seemed too happy to get the assignment by a film producer to rewrite me. His personal life was much like mine: born-and-raised New Yorker, single, and also just like me, wrote novels, plays, and television scripts.

Though we shared many similar traits, in my eyes Warren had no backbone as a human being, no original artistic vision, and no interesting literary style. However, he had won some major theatrical and television awards and was paid better than I was.

He was short and slightly built, quick-witted, charming, and pretended to be erudite, though like me, he was from humble beginnings. He had a mass of curly black hair, very tiny dark brown eyes, and a melodious voice.

If you liked him, he appeared to be a sweet-natured cherub with a wiggle in his walk; if you didn't like him, he was more like an eyeless, underground mole who dealt with the dirt producers threw at writers by eating it with a hearty appetite. I was his competition and he was mine, so despite any charm he might have possessed, I saw him and knew him as the latter.

I never trusted Warren Fabrizi; Sarah, my longtime thirty-five year old girlfriend who lived in a small apartment on Grove Street in the West Village and was an editor at a fashion magazine, sometimes remarked that I was jealous of him. Actually, I felt he was jealous of me, but then again, we were both writers competing for the attention of our agent, an audience, and studio producers. In another time and another world, we would have been sworn enemies fighting each other with rocks and swords. But he didn't have to worry about me anymore. I died.

It was a stroke that killed me a little before noon. People have them all the time without any reaction, but mine just happened in the wrong place when an artery in my neck got clogged by a piece of cholesterol that broke off the artery wall. I felt pain for a few seconds on the right side of my body but I thought it was just a muscle spasm, because I'd been at the gym that morning.

My super found me that night when he came by to check on a leak in my bathroom that was causing water to flood the apartment beneath mine. The coroner's office deemed it thrombosis or, more likely, an embolism. The rest is history, or more accurately, nothing more than a mention in the *Daily News* obituary column because they recognized my name. I was all of forty-four years old.

I had expected to live way into my eighties, like my senile father who was happily enjoying the twilight of his life in an assisted living home in Riverhead, Long Island, or at the very least into my midseventies, like my mother before she lost her bout with cancer.

Dying at the age of forty-four with two published novels, eight published plays, and four shared screenplay credits on IMDb was far from what I had expected concerning my life's work. My entire writing career was ahead of me, or so I'd thought. I had plans for another play, eventually other novels. All were going to be monumental stories with important cultural themes, which made me daydream about winning first a Pulitzer, later on the Nobel Prize. I'd also thought that with more artistic success under my belt, maybe I'd settle down and get married to Sarah, yet an artistic success was a novel that most critics loved but in general, nobody outside of your friends, ever read.

I'd been teaching film writing part-time, adjunct, at CUNY and NYU and had taken all the necessary steps to become famous in my lifetime. I had a clear career path, as they say. I had no baggage. I'd never married and never had children in order to ensure that life's detours didn't distract me. I made money from studio and network writing assignments, I had a successful agent (nearly an impossibility), and I was smart enough to save my money, not spend it all on a big house in Santa Monica after I sold my first screenplay only to never work again and lose it all. I had heard of so many writers—those who lived on the edge, who did rewrite work—who were deemed too old for the studios when they turned fifty and weren't hired anymore. I swore I wouldn't become one of them, but of course dying at my age made this irrelevant.

I'd been living in a modest fifth-floor apartment in the trendy Williamsburg section of Brooklyn, gliding nicely along, considering myself at my peak when it came to the true understanding of plot, story, and theme. Hell, I was right there. I had learned the three-act structure format so well it had become part of my DNA.

I was a member of the Writers Guild of America, East; the Authors Guild; the Dramatists Guild of America; Poets & Writers; and PEN International. I was, in the most specific definition possible, an artistic success.

My first novel, *The Last Vision,* was about an aging and lonely poet's last day of life as he roams the streets of his small Long Island town, struggling to complete a poem he has spent ten years writing. When the clock strikes midnight he completes the poem and then commits suicide by throwing himself in front of a Long Island Rail Road commuter train on the Port Jefferson line. *Publishers Weekly* and *Kirkus Reviews* gave it rave reviews; *The New Yorker* actually called it "brilliant."

My second novel, *The Dead Mexican*, was the story of an illegal immigrant from Oaxaca who is murdered by a racist cop in a small town in upstate New York; his young wife sneaks into the country to find his murderer. *The New York Times* called it a "masterpiece of social comment and intrigue."

But that was then and this is now. And now I'm no longer in existence. I don't need to tell you about the wake or the funeral or that my grave is in Calvary, a big cemetery in Queens. Those are incidentals. What is important is that I learned a lot about immortality *after* dying, because no one knows much about it before you die.

I was one of those who craved immortality and thought that perhaps a little notoriety on Earth would bring some fame after my demise. There was nothing wrong with that notion, or so I thought. And then, like I keep saying, I ruined it all by actually dying.

CHAPTER 2

Time moves quickly after you die. Your wake, your funeral, the burial ceremony–they all feel like a movie trailer you watch without emotion. Faces, names seem trivial; time is insignificant. I saw Sarah standing at my grave. She was crying and she was holding my father's hand. He seemed to be enjoying what was going on and probably had no idea why he was standing in the cemetery. Dementia reigned supreme in his existence. My agent, Claudia Wilson, never showed up nor did any of my friends, but because I didn't have any really close friends, I wasn't too upset.

After your burial, the next time you are aware of anything, you are someplace you've never been before.

A young man in his late twenties told me I was now in the Writers Afterlife. We were sitting together on a wooden bench on a hill. There was a wonderful breeze, the sun felt early morning–like, and my surroundings were really quiet.

"Call me Joe," he said. He was trim, small-boned, with a slight beard and shoulder-length hair. He wore a silk white shirt trimmed with silver, a gold cross, and several rings. One onyx ring could have been from Persia and the other ebony ring from Greece. He had sandals on his feet and loose black trousers. "So, as you no doubt surmised by now, you're dead. You've passed on to a place all writers go to after they die."

I listened closely. He had a soothing voice.

"You probably have a lot of questions and that's fine. Everyone, no matter who they are, has questions. But first you will be given an ovation for living a writer's life."

"An ovation? For real?" I asked.

"For real," he assured, "it's the Writers Afterlife."

I suddenly found myself on a large outdoor stage, sitting on a chair facing an audience of thousands. Colorful banners waved in the wind and there was an orchestra playing from someplace I couldn't see.

Joe appeared at my side. "Take a bow."

I stood up, walked to center stage, and faced the thousands of strangers who were smiling in an anticipation of something. I wondered who could be in the audience . . . any family? My mother was dead. My agent couldn't be there and neither could any of my competition on Earth. I wondered if any of the great members of the literary elite were seated facing me.

"They're expecting a speech," Joe said.

"I don't have one prepared," I told him.

"We know," he said, then handed me a piece of paper and disappeared behind me.

I looked down at the paper and there was a pre-written speech on it. I read aloud the large, bold print. "My name is Tom Chillo and I've spend most of my life as a writer."

I heard applause.

I continued reading. "Poetry changed my life while I was still a teenager. Then when I grew older all books did. I read every novel I could find."

The crowd applauded again.

"In college I saw plays and loved reading them, then eventually writing them. I had always written poetry or so it seemed. After graduate school I wrote screenplays. Writers are born, not made. Writing is a vocation, not a vacation. Thank you for listening." I bowed. It was all

true and I felt a sense of accomplishment as the crowd
not only applauded but cheered. I saw hundreds and
hundreds of happy faces sitting in chairs on the green
manicured lawn that rolled out into the distance bigger
than a football field and in all directions.

The audience seemed to care about everything I said.
Some stood up when I was done and gave me a standing
ovation just as I was promised. I was amazed at my own
charm and sense of presence at that moment.

There was also a Q&A where the audience asked me
about my work. We discussed my plays and how they
were influenced by my notion that it was my mission to
record the story of life and how it occurred on my
planet—the boroughs of Queens and Brooklyn. I told
the audience how I could hear my characters specifically
as they spoke and how their dialogue revealed who they
were, their aspirations and their dreams, as well as their
disappointments and failures.

I also told them that it was important to have my characters vibrate with insecurities. Hamlet was like that; so
was Jay Gatsby, and my favorite film character, the
charming and good-looking Edward "Fast Eddie" Felson
in *The Hustler.* The most memorable characters always
have a flaw that makes them vibrate with deep vulnera-
bility. The audience participated with enthusiasm and

great appreciation for all my work. They laughed at my quips and seemed delighted to know the inner workings of my craft.

"So, do you have any questions?" I heard a voice ask.

Joe and I were sitting on a grassy hill overlooking a river that stretched into the horizon. The crowd, the stage, the colorful banners were all gone.

"Where did everybody go?" I asked.

"Oh, they were only there for your speech. Your speech was over, so they left."

"Just like that?"

"Oh yeah."

"They seemed so enthused. Were they real?"

He smirked but then quickly changed his attitude. "They were for *you*."

This explained nothing.

"So, questions?"

My moment on stage giving my speech had really moved me. "I really made it, then?"

Joe nodded. "Yes, you did. You are now in the Writers Afterlife. Congratulations."

I smiled. I was happy and then I blurted out, "Am I famous?"

"No," he quickly answered.

I felt as if I'd been punched in the stomach.

"What else?" Joe asked. "Anything else you want to know?"

"Is my work admired?" I asked.

"No more than it was when you were living," he said.

"That's it? I mean all my hard work, all my dreams, all my dedication, and that's it? I spent my life writing and I'm not famous?"

"Sorry," he said, though I doubted he meant it.

"Will I become famous?"

"Hard to tell."

"Was it because I died young? Or that I didn't write enough?"

"Well, perhaps. William Butler Yeats wrote his greatest poem, "The Circus Animals' Desertion," when he was in his seventh decade. Voltaire wrote *Candide* when he was sixty-four. William Shakespeare wrote his greatest work after he was forty-four."

"I'm forty-four."

"You *died* at forty-four." He forced a smile. "Anything else?"

I was getting annoyed. "Hold on. Can you not rush me?"

"Take your time," he said. He leaned back on his hands. We were sitting on a blanket. He looked around. I could tell he was bored.

"Am I boring you?"

Joe shook his head quickly and sincerely said, "Not at all."

"It's not fair."

"Yes. Bad luck on your part. However, you did have your chance. John Keats died at twenty-six. Percy Bysshe Shelley hardly reached thirty and Lord Byron just passed thirty. And the list goes on for those who wrote wonderful things before forty-four including Nathaniel Hawthorne, Dante. And don't forget Dante was *only* fifty-six years old when he died. And Shakespeare was fifty-two!"

"Stop," I said. "Forty-four is young. It's too young to die."

"Once again, compared with what? With whom? The Brontë sisters all died very young, and so did Jane Austen. Vincent van Gogh was only thirty-seven."

"I don't care how young these people are. In my world forty-four is young. Imagine what I could have written if I had lived another decade. If I had lived another two decades. I might have written a masterpiece if I had lived longer."

"Perhaps," Joe responded dryly. "But you're dead, Tom. There's nothing you can do about that now."

"I could have eaten better, worked out more, prayed . . . whatever."

"Not sure if any of that would have made that much of a difference in the long run. What's a few more years in the larger scheme of things? Whatever you think you might have written or imagined you might have created if you'd had more time is irrelevant now. You were young at one time. You had the opportunity and you did write two wonderful novels and several terrific plays. Be satisfied with that," Joe told me with an odd sense of empathy, as if he had been there himself.

"So, we agree that inspiration does hit many when they are young and some when they are old. Let's move on, shall we?" He shrugged his shoulders and stood. "Okay, so my duty is to greet you, explain some details about the Writers Afterlife so you can move on into your future."

"I have a future?"

He smiled. "Of course you do. You paid your dues. You will live rent free and nearly pain free. You will want very little, you will never get tired, you will never experience hunger, you will never miss anyone. In other words, you will lose all the awful things human beings suffer, for the rest of eternity."

I almost bought into his sales pitch but one part bothered me. "You said I will live *nearly* pain free. You said 'nearly.'"

Joe shook his head. "That's right. There is one tiny unpleasantness you will experience."

"And what is that?"

"An acute sense of anxiety."

"From?"

"Never being famous."

Again I felt as if someone hit me in the stomach. "For how long?"

"For eternity, I'm sorry to say."

As you'd expect, I was stunned, but Joe managed to motivate me to walk with him to shake off the disappointment. So I walked in silence across the hill. I eventually realized he was giving me a subtle tour of my new home. It was beautiful and green with lovely trees and a blue sky with dancing clouds. The sun felt warm on my face and he was absolutely right. I didn't miss anyone or anything. I had no regrets. I felt as if the burden of living life had been lifted from my entire being. I was elated and nearly felt light-footed when I walked. All was perfect, as if I were in heaven, except one thing that nagged at me like a tooth that was slowly aching.

"Are you sure I'll never become a famous writer, posthumously?"

"It's hard to say," he quickly stated. "Some up here actually did."

"I could be one of those writers."

"You could."

"I did write some damn good things."

"You certainly did."

"You agree they were good?"

Joe kept walking. "I haven't read them myself, you know, but the word up here is that you had talent and you dedicated yourself to that talent with hard work. But remember, not all in the universe is explainable. Some things just stay a mystery. I mean, I can conjure for you some reasons everything is against your becoming famous after your death, but you probably are aware of them.

"One truth is this: if you *had* lived another twenty years, you might have written a masterpiece. You might have written it and then died and still achieved fame. Niccolò Machiavelli was a playwright and a writer and he died before his masterpiece, *The Prince*, was ever published—and look, he's famous. His name is actually an adjective. Also, if you had lived longer, you might have met someone who'd have made sure your work was produced and published to more critical acclaim. But you, my dear, dead Tom Chillo, must accept the fact that fame slipped by because of your bad fortune."

I was sullen. The beautiful landscape surrounding me was suddenly meaningless. "I'm sad."

"You will be sad for eternity, I'm sorry to say. You will suffer the anxiety of a missed opportunity until the ever-expanding universe stops expanding and just . . . *ends*."

CHAPTER 3

Time in the Writers Afterlife is very different from time on Earth. It has no exact purpose; day and night seem to change as if by whim. The days and nights are splendid. The breeze is cool, and the sun shines with warmth without ever getting hot. In the evening the moon is white and magnificent and the stars gleam through wisps of clouds. After a short while I realized that each individual writer creates the exterior landscape he or she is in by imagining it. If you think night, it's night. If you think of a city, there it is. The Afterlife is truly fueled by each writer's imagination.

One quiet night Joe told me a little about himself. He had been a painter born in Florence in 1578, and had wanted to be famous like Michelangelo. He'd made his way to Rome where he found nothing but indifference to his work. He sold a few paintings but not nearly enough to pay for a roof over his head. After several years, he gave up, married a farmer's daughter, and moved to a small farm north of Rome where he toiled until his death from plague when he was only forty-four.

"You wanted to be famous?"

"Like hundreds of painters and sculptors who entered Rome's barred gates every year. I wanted to be Michelangelo. I burned with the need for fame. I dreamt of being the stuff of legend."

"And it didn't happen?"

"Did you ever hear of the great painter Gianni Palmintieri Guiliano?" he asked.

I shook my head.

And that was why Joe had been assigned me: he was a good painter but never famous on Earth, and we had also died at the same age. Whoever did the assigning, and that was never brought up, thought Joe and I would be a good match.

Joe told me he tried not to think about his life on Earth, so he tried not to talk about it. He told me that he too felt an overwhelming sadness, and that many of those who just missed out on being famous were eventually asked to be Afterlife tour guides. Each one was given an artist who had just missed being famous and had been the same age at the time of death. Tour guides eased their charges into their particular afterlives, just as Joe was doing for me. He told me that I'd probably be assigned an actor or perhaps a composer but certainly not a writer. That was how it worked. You guided someone you couldn't compete with but had empathy for.

He also told me that in time I'd get used to existence in the Writers Afterlife. The good news was I'd never get a cold or flu. I'd never get even a pimple. I'd never have sexual desire or the need to be romantically in love.

"How about the urge to write?" I asked.

"Gone for all eternity," he said smiling widely.

That notion bothered me for a moment, but then the slight twinge of sorrow passed. I had written my entire life. I didn't have much memory of ever not being a writer. It was going to be weird not getting up and planning my day around writing *something*.

We walked a few more minutes or weeks; I had no notion how *long* our walk actually took when I saw a woman off in the distance. She stood on a hill, in the wind, and the sky above her was a dark and foreboding wilderness. Her long, dark hair flew wildly over her shoulder and she was wearing clothing that made her look like a poor woman from the mid-nineteenth century.

The closer we got to her, the more I could see. Now there was drizzling rain; the landscape around her looked like a moor. The kind of moor you'd find in the England of *Wuthering Heights*.

I stopped. "Emily Brontë?"

"Excellent. You know your writers," Joe replied. "She's one of the Eternals I wanted you to meet."

"Can I meet her?" I asked.

"Go ahead. Go over to her," he told me.

I walked ahead and suddenly I was in her world. I was on the hill, feeling the drizzle on my face. I felt the wind blowing and watched her standing there looking off into the distance. As I drew closer, I noticed an aura around her. She was radiant, a contrast to the gloomy landscape surrounding her. I edged up to her from the side and saw that even though she was alone, she didn't look lonely. I felt that despite her large dark and sad eyes, she was exuding warmth and contentment. Her long-sleeved, light-blue dress covered her from her neck to her ankles.

She turned to me and said without smiling, "Thank you so much."

"For what?"

"For reading me," she answered.

"It was my pleasure, Miss Brontë," I said.

"Call me Emily," she replied, barely thirty years old and immortal. Then she turned away from me and smiled to the figure of a man, a shadow, walking out of the mist of the moor depicting her sexual longing. He was handsome with longish hair blowing in the same breeze, wet from the same drizzle falling, and he had the same sparkle in his eyes that she had.

It was Heathcliff. I stepped back. They embraced.

I turned and caught a glimpse of Joe, who was standing in a streak of light that separated the moor from where I had previously been. Joe nodded to me. I understood. I got it. Emily Brontë would live through eternity with the perfect male of her own creation. She and Heathcliff would be romantic lovers as long as there was a thing called time.

I walked back to Joe. "So that's her joy. That's her reward," I told him.

Joe nodded. "Not far from here is Charlotte Brontë, who will be forever happy with her Rochester."

I saw them suddenly. She was on a bench, knitting, and he was sitting at her side. There was an enormous mansion on a hill above them. Charlotte *was* Jane Eyre, and it all was beginning to make sense.

Joe urged me to follow him. "There are more writers for you to meet. Let's meet the others. The other Eternals."

CHAPTER 4

You can imagine how I felt when I first saw Shakespeare. Joe and I entered this open-air stage, which I immediately recognized as the Globe Theatre. William was standing front and center surrounded by Hamlet, Ophelia, King Lear, Macbeth, Lady Macbeth, Rosalind, Romeo and his Juliet, Othello, Iago, Puck, Falstaff, and all the others.

There was laughter and food everywhere, beer and wine, and in the middle of it all was Shakespeare himself with a big smile on his face.

"To be or not to be!" Hamlet shouted. All the other characters laughed. They handed bottles of wine back and forth, portions of chicken and goose. It was a picnic. I realized William Shakespeare would be having a picnic with all of his characters through the rest of time.

"Hey, Lear!" he shouted. "Who is the Fool now?"

Lear beamed. If fact, all the characters beamed when Shakespeare called to them. He had created them. He had made them as real as human beings.

I could hardly move when that thought struck me. I spoke but I couldn't take my eyes off the great playwright. "He seems happy beyond words."

"Oh, he is," Joe stated, with a twinge of sadness in his voice.

I watched as Ophelia sat on Shakespeare's lap feeding him grapes and Puck ran his hands through Shakespeare's thinning hair. Hamlet handed him a goblet of wine as all turned to Macbeth, who now took center stage and said, "Tomorrow and tomorrow and tomorrow . . . ," performing the world-famous monologue for all the other characters.

"He was lucky, you know," Joe told me.

We were then joined by Romeo and Juliet who had seen us and slipped away from the others. They were a perfect couple wearing bright colors perfect for Renaissance Italy.

"His wisdom is profound when it comes to human nature," Romeo said. He took Juliet's hand. "Have you met my Juliet before?" he asked me.

I found myself looking into the lovely eyes of literature's loveliest young woman, barely just a teenager, and I was smitten. Her large eyes, beaming with intelligence and curiosity, drew me to her.

"Never in person," I said.

"You are a playwright too, kind sir?" she asked.

"I am. But I'm no Bard of Avon."

"No one is. But not all have to be to share their gifts with theater."

"That was sweet of you to say."

Juliet took my hand and I nearly fell over. Her own hand was soft and tiny. She then leaned to Romeo and kissed his cheek. She spun around and the two of them ran off like two teenagers in love, which was exactly what they were.

"My God, how the hell did he create such a masterpiece of a human heart?" I asked.

Joe again urged me to continue walking and we left the theater. "Lots of talent, but like I said before, he was lucky."

"Who was lucky?"

"Shakespeare. He had an advocate after he died."

"I didn't know that."

"Oh yes. For fifty years after his death, no one really thought he was a great playwright. It wasn't until someone bailed the great critic Samuel Johnson out of debtors' prison and hired him to write a critical study of Shakespeare's work that Willie became famous."

"Who hired Johnson?"

"Jacob Tonson. That you can easily find out in a history book. The real question is, who cajoled and then persuaded Tonson to hire Johnson?"

I was enthralled with this new information.

"More about all that later. But now would you like to meet Willie?"

Moments later I was on stage facing the great playwright while standing under the bright sunshine that was pouring through the ceiling.

Shakespeare had the charisma of a movie star, I thought to myself as I smiled at him. I wondered, though, if it was being famous that made him appear that way. He was a thin, tiny man with a sparkling smile.

"I was once hired to do a rewrite of an adaptation of one your plays for Warner Brothers," I told him.

"Excellent," he said, quickly eying Ophelia as he spoke to me.

"It was a modernized version of *A Midsummer Night's Dream.*" I continued to smile.

"Good," he said again, this time taking Ophelia by the hand and placing her back on his lap.

Rosalind stepped forward and kissed Willie on the lips. There was more laughter, and then she turned and Shakespeare ran after her across the stage, disappearing into the wings, with the beautiful Ophelia following in pursuit.

"Like I said, a lucky man," I heard Joe say. I listened closely as Joe went on to remind me that no one thought Shakespeare was great until Jacob Tonson mysteriously hired Samuel Johnson to write a history of the literary importance of Willie. Up until then the world thought Ben Johnson was the Elizabethan era's great playwright.

Just then, Joe stopped and nodded to an Elizabethan gentleman sitting alone on a bench outside the theater. He was looking up at the Globe, brooding. "There he is. The *forgotten* Ben Johnson."

I inched my way over to him. There was a metaphoric as well as a literal cloud of gloom hanging over the man's head.

When I was right beside Ben Johnson, he turned to me and his look said everything. Though he was dressed in the finest clothing of his time, with gold bracelets and emerald rings on his fingers, he was sad. His time for fame had come and gone and now all he could do was hope that sometime in the future of literature, he would be considered a great playwright and poet.

Christopher Marlowe popped up from behind a tree. I already knew a lot about him; he'd been a friend of Shakespeare's and had died in his twenties. He was murdered in a bar and he might have been a spy of some kind for the queen of England. His *Faust*, though not as long as Johann Wolfgang von Goethe's, was pretty well known. He was one of those who'd died just as he was becoming famous.

"You see, up here, there are Eternals; there are those who were famous while on Earth and now forgotten; and there are those who are, like you on the verge," Joe said.

"The verge," I repeated.

"Those who died before fame happened. Christopher Marlowe is more famous than you think and that too came after his death."

We watched the handsome, young, and carefree Marlowe running through the trees, seemingly drunk, followed by several other handsome young men as care-free and seemingly as drunk. Their voices quickly disappeared.

"He seems happy."

"Well, in his instance graduate students keep him famous. He did write some famous lines. And I guess that's fame enough for him. Think about it, his competition is Shakespeare and Marlowe did die at twenty-nine."

"'Who ever loved, that loved not at first sight?'" I quickly added.

"The majority of writers here fall into the last category: on the verge, those who tried and failed, and wait in the Valley of Those on the Verge in hopes of one day becoming an Eternal. There are thousands of you like that."

"So it can happen?" I asked.

"Yes. It does happen."

"Emily Dickinson only published seven poems in her lifetime. Think about that! She is now considered the most famous woman poet of all time," Joe said.

"How did that happen for her?" I asked.

"After Emily died, her sister, Lavinia, collected all of her poetry in a book and sent it to a publisher."

"Wow." I sighed.

"And Franz Kafka! He was virtually unknown when he died and told his friends to burn all of his work. In fact, his *Metamorphosis* was the only thing he ever completed and it was very short for a novel," Joe continued. "It was his friend Max Brod who made sure Kafka's work was published after he died. Now there's the Franz Kafka Society Center in Prague."

I took it all in, not knowing any of this when I was alive.

"So yes, it can happen for those who are lucky to have someone care about their work after they die—and for those who go back to influence at least one person who is still alive and can make the difference."

I was stunned. "We can influence those still alive?"

Joe nodded. "Yes, you have one chance, one opportunity to go back to life and do all you can to change the fate of your fame."

We walked on. I was perplexed, and Joe could see it. "It's all very complicated," he said, "and you will learn all the details in time."

CHAPTER 5

"Who is that?" I asked as Joe and I walked along the sidewalk of a big city somewhere in the twentieth century. I'd just noticed a middle-aged man sitting alone in a park.

Naturally the city was deserted and only an illusion, as was all that existed in the Writers Afterlife. Joe nodded. "Sad story, his," he replied. "He had five best sellers in America in the early twentieth century. He was the first person to ever make a million dollars for writing fiction. He was very wealthy and very, very popular. Only Charles Dickens and Sir Walter Scott have had more best sellers in the English language before him."

"Who is he?"

"You wouldn't even recognized his name if I told you."

"Really?"

"Fifteen movies were based on his stories. Gary Cooper and John Wayne starred in two of them. He wrote plays and published nineteen novels. Hardly anyone reads his work anymore."

"Please tell me who he is."

"Harold Bell Wright," Joe told me.

"Who?"

"Exactly."

I was wobbly with all the information.

As we walked by I noticed the man look up at us. He spoke up, and his voice still echoes in my head. "Do you read me?" he asked.

Joe hurried me along. "Don't respond. Whatever you say will be the wrong answer."

Suddenly we were in another city, and another man was at a table alone sipping champagne with music from the Roaring Twenties floating through the air. A yellow Rolls-Royce was parked beside his table and he was eating caviar. The scene struck me as odd, as the man was alone yet trying to act as if he were surrounded by friends and adoring fans.

"Do you see that man there?"

I could very clearly see the slender man with thick hair, thick eyebrows, and a bushy mustache dressed impeccably in a grandiose suit and tie, doing all he could to make it obvious to anyone looking that he was enjoying himself.

"Who is he?" I asked, looking closely.

"He had a best seller the year *The Great Gatsby* was published. Every high school student knows that novel; hardly anyone alive remembers his," Joe told me.

"What was it titled?"

"*The Green Hat*. It was about the same world of the Roaring Twenties as *Gatsby* but it lacked the style, execution, language, and perhaps the great storytelling of F. Scott Fitzgerald. But that author, he was on the cover of *Time* magazine!"

"The cover of *Time* magazine?" I repeated. "But I don't know him," I said. I said it too loudly, and the man looked at me with a deep sadness in his big, dark eyes, then looked away from us both.

"Michael Arlen," Joe whispered his name. "The last ten years of his life he suffered from writers block and didn't write a word. A few years after he died, he was nearly forgotten."

I shrugged my shoulders. I remembered a saying I knew back when I was alive: "A best seller is the gilded tomb of a mediocre talent." I turned to Joe. "So are we saying that the mediocre talents who are famous when alive fade into obscurity once time catches up with them?"

Joe shrugged. "Not entirely true but there's a better chance of that happening than someone living in obscurity and being discovered later on."

As we left the city I looked over my shoulder and there he sat on the park bench, the only man in the entire metropolis. He sat there for all eternity with the tall buildings as a backdrop. In a city of thousands, no one knew him. Though he felt no hunger, no lust, no need for sleep, and no fear of death, he did feel the deep anxiety and sense of loss of fame, now all but ignored.

Joe leaned in and said to me, "Henry David Thoreau had Ralph Waldo Emerson. This poor guy has no one. But there are so many wonderful writers of some wonderful books that no one knows or reads today and their books were not best sellers by a long shot," he said. He noticed a man sitting at another park bench with a very thick moustache. He had eyes like dark beams of light and wavy hair combed back. "That's George Gissing, a writer from the 1890s," Joe told me. "His book *The Odd Women* is well loved."

I had never heard of it.

Joe then gestured to a woman walking through the park. "There's Olivia Manning. Her book *School for Love* got her up here."

I thought I had heard of the book but wasn't sure.

"We'll see if she becomes an Eternal," he said.

We walked around and Joe pointed out other writers to me. "There's F. M. Mayor. She died when she was sixty, having never married after the man she was engaged to died of typhoid fever in India. Her *Rector's Daughter* is considered a neglected classic," Joe told me. "I enjoyed it, but it is such a devastating story of love lost."

F. M. Mayor sat at the base of the Taj Mahal with a young, handsome British soldier who I thought must be her husband. She was reading her novel to him, and they looked happy despite the storyline.

Suddenly we were in Bermuda and I saw an interesting-looking woman sitting by a swimming pool, typing and wearing her sunglasses. "Who is she?"

"Oh, that is Elisabeth Sanxay Holding. She wrote *The Blank Wall* and Raymond Chandler called her the best detective and suspense writer of them all." Joe grinned. "Look out for her."

"What do you mean?"

"They just made a movie of her book a couple of years ago. She may actually make it out of the Valley of Those on the Verge."

That's when we saw an interesting statue. It was of an old man and it was in the middle of a square. The old man was asleep and looked a little like someone who had eaten a sour grape. "Who's that?"

"Henry Roth," Joe answered. "He wrote *Call It Sleep*. An American classic."

"A great book no one reads," I said. I looked at the marble statue. "Why is this here?"

"Well, Henry Roth wrote that wonderful novel, then he had the longest writer's block in history. He had no interest in being famous, so when he died and first came here he built this statue as a reminder to all writers that fame is not the point. Then he went to the place where ordinary people go when they die and has never been seen since," Joe told me.

I had had enough of writers who almost, might, and/or never will make it to the hill where the Eternals dwelled. "Take me to the Eternals, please," I asked.

—m—

Leo Tolstoy was impressive. We found him standing on this huge archway in the center of a snow-covered field. Thousands of his admirers were sitting facing him on all sides of the archway reading *War and Peace* in unison, in Russian. It was so dramatic, so filled with great words, gloom and doom. Tolstoy looked like a prophet up there in the swirling snow, mouthing the words as his readers held their heads down in his enormous book.

"Very cool," I said.

Joe smirked. "The Eternals have some peculiar needs. Would you believe Tolstoy hasn't moved since he got here? That enormous crowd reads everything of his over and over again, and he just listens without a single reaction. But you can tell he loves every moment of it."

Watching John Keats was a lovely experience. He sat on a small hill under a row of trees with golden leaves. It was autumn, and he was reading a small book of his own poetry; sitting beside him was a young woman as petite as he. I was beginning to realize that so many of the writers I had come across were small-boned men and women.

Keats looked like a child to me, yet managed to be elegant in his fame. Everything around him was so perfectly put together: the bushes, the green grass, and the golden trees. His companion had auburn hair and as they sat together on a blanket, she frequently smiled. I realized as we got closer that Keats was reading aloud his poetry to her, and she was listening intently. They held hands as he read.

We soon came upon Mary Shelley who was running wildly in the same woods, followed by Victor Frankenstein and the monster. But they were all laughing; there wasn't any fear or anxiety in any of them.

I did notice that Mary was naked and her very pale English skin gleamed in the bright sunlight. Percy Shelley was not far away; he was lecturing a crowd of college-age coeds and he looked like a rock star as his lovely wife ran naked through the throng of his admirers. They seemed in love, though, as if they were spending eternity in a very odd sexual tease, happy despite their being competitive and so very famous.

Lord Byron was sitting on a rock below a Grecian ruin. He had curly hair and looked as if he had just finished playing a gig up in Woodstock. He was reading "She Walks in Beauty" to a small crowd of very sophisticated men and women all dressed as if it were the early nineteenth century. They gave the impression that listening to this poet read was all they wanted. As I drew closer, I saw that Byron had put heavy makeup on his face, which made him look more brooding and near death despite the big smile he had on his face and all his fans sitting at his feet.

Charles Dickens was also a petite man who hurried through the London streets followed by two happy boys: Oliver Twist and David Copperfield. Joe and I followed Dickens into a large theater and watched him step onto the stage. In a few minutes he began to recite his own prose to the large crowd. He'd always been one of my favorite novelists and there he was, on stage reading his own work sounding like a pretentiously bad actor, but who cared? The audience was just happy to see him in person as he read aloud and acted out the characters of Uriah Heap, Pip, Amy Dorrit, Cratchit, Estella, Morley, and my all-time favorite, Ebenezer Scrooge.

And there in the front row were David and Oliver, living for every word Dickens pronounced. I sighed with gratification to see such a great talent being idolized in the Afterlife.

Just a few moments later, I came up on Lorraine Hansberry. She wrote one of my favorite plays, *A Raisin in the Sun,* and was the first black woman to have her play produced on Broadway. She was only in her mid-thirties when she died. There she was in the back of a Broadway theater watching a young man who I was sure was the character Walter Lee Younger.

"I always wanted to meet you," I whispered to her.

She turned to me and shook my hand but didn't say a word. I could see that she lived for every moment she had written. I was close enough to hear that she was not only mouthing the words as Tolstoy had done, but whispering them aloud.

At the intermission she stood in the middle of a crowd who barely acknowledged her and said to me, "I'm so happy to spend every night of eternity as if it were opening night. They will love the play and they will give it awards and though I will die soon, I am so happy. So very, very happy."

I nodded.

"And I just love that young man."

The lights blinked and she quickly went to her place in the back of the theater to watch her play and keep her eternal love of her wonderful character Walter Lee Younger in her heart and line of vision for all time.

Meeting Eugene O'Neill was quite interesting. He was in a bar, which made sense; he was drunk, which made sense, and he was sitting with the Tyrone family. I saw Mary and James and Jamie and Edmund all drinking with him. Well, Mary didn't drink as much but she looked a bit dazed.

It was interesting how they all seemed taken with one another, though they never truly looked into one another's faces. Only James looked right at O'Neill and said, "Look up at me, Eugene. Look me in the eye, son," though James wasn't much older, if he was even older at all. I could see that O'Neill himself was quite happy being in the glow of his family, possibly his real family, possibly his own fictionalized version of himself as well for all time and forever, et cetera.

I could even see a slight smile come to his face, when James recited a line from *Long Day's Journey into Night* with a booming regional actor's voice and filled the dingy bar on Manhattan's Lower East Side. It was a play itself, watching the great playwright enjoying his own private hell. Also, somehow in the moment, I could see with my own eyes that O'Neill's writing the play was clearly therapeutic and eased the agony of that hell—making it, in a way, a bit of heavenly comfort.

Joe and I found Samuel Beckett in what looked like a no-man's-land of the First World War, leaning against a crumbling tree with a ray of sunlight lighting up his face. He seemed content while alone with his thoughts.

William Faulkner sat under a large willow tree, sipping a drink, dressed in a suit and tie. He was elegant, plain, and simple with his neatly trimmed mustache and his smoothly combed gray hair. He was alone, facing an Underwood typewriter, on serene display as if he were rarified and hailed. Indeed, his likeness adorned a U.S. postage stamp and he had won a Nobel Prize, which sat on display beside him. There was no hint of sound or fury in the Writers Afterlife for him. Though a heavy drinker, Faulkner never drank while he wrote and now that he was dead, he didn't seem to allow chaos to intrude on his place in immortality.

I also got to see Robert Penn Warren, the only writer to win Pulitzer Prizes for both poetry and fiction. He was at an old-fashioned picnic enjoying himself as if he were Willie Stark in *All the King's Men.*

Mark Twain was not far off but though he was one of the Eternals, he didn't glow in a warm light nor did he seem content or happy like the others. There was a cloud of sadness around him, a sense of tragedy that made no sense to me.

"He is thrilled to be here because of his literary recognition, but the sorrows of his personal life never seemed to leave him even in death," Joe explained.

This is not what I expected of the man who was so famous for his erudite and self-deprecating quips, along with *Adventures of Huckleberry Finn* and *The Adventures of Tom Sawyer.*

That's when I saw a small but handsome and suntanned young man with sharp, dark eyes pacing back and forth, looking very anxiously around. "Who's that?"

"Oh, that's John Fante. He got asked up not long ago. He was in the Valley for a bit of time."

"Yes, he wrote *Ask the Dust*!" I proclaimed. "He wrote some screenplays too, but I only learned about him when I was in Rome and found out that the Italians really love him," I said.

Joe nodded. "Charles Bukowski helped get him into the Eternals. In fact, *Time Out* recently wrote it was 'criminal negligence' that *Ask the Dust* isn't better known." Joe walked on. After I caught up with him, he continued, "What's interesting is that Fante got in, but look at Nelson Algren. His novel *The Man with the Golden Arm* was made into a movie starring Frank Sinatra. He was one of the most famous writers of his time. Fought his way up from working-class Chicago and was so respected in his lifetime. And now who knows his name? Who?"

"I do."

"That's my point. You're another writer."

I walked over to Fante. He had picked his early twenties to be in while dwelling in the land of the Eternals. He was sitting on a beach, sipping a beer, expressionless, surrounded by pretty Mexican women. I was curious about that blank look on his face so I had to introduce myself. "How did it feel when you heard your name called?" I asked.

He eased back in his lounge chair and said, "It was the most exhilarating moment of my existence."

"Anything you can share with me?" I asked.

His windswept hair blew across his forehead and the sun rubbed light across his strong features.

"Time spent in the Valley of Those on the Verge is time spent in hell," he answered. "Living was a picnic compared with that place."

I lowered my head and snuck away.

The last writer we saw also surprised me. He was sitting behind the wheel of a 1955 royal-blue Packard Clipper convertible. He was a thirty-year-old Jack Kerouac, tanned with a sharp jaw, a crew-cut, and a nerdy look that was very hip back in the fifties. I heard jazz playing from all around the car as it sat there doing fifty miles an hour without moving. Anything was possible here in the Writers Afterlife. Ironically, Kerouac never got a driver's license when he was alive.

He was on the road, a highway actually, where the sun reigned over a cloudless sky. Everything about him was at ease, relaxed and serene now that he had made it. He was an icon of the Beat Generation, probably more famous than any of the others. He looked slim and healthy, nothing like that bloated body he inhabited when he died of cirrhosis of the liver at the age of forty-seven, having lived only three years longer than I had.

I expected to see Neal Cassady in the seat beside him or a few pretty girls he'd picked up as he drove across America but I was shocked when I saw his mother, Gabrielle, sitting in the backseat. He looked comforted and sedate. From where I stood, I could see that his round light-blue eyes filled with happiness.

I looked at Joe and said, "I bet he's the only Eternal who sits in a car."

Eventually Joe led me to a very strange place in the Writers Afterlife. It was where all the writers who'd committed suicide were.

"This is an odd place, so if you feel uneasy, it's not you, it's the place itself," Joe assured me.

We were in a garden with so many colorful flowers and small trees and bushes everywhere. The garden had some metal and marble fountains and an occasional metal table and chair. Some writers sat at these tables and others milled around the garden.

I quickly recognized Sylvia Plath, Anne Sexton, and Ernest Hemingway, and then Thomas Chatterton and Sir John Suckling from famous portraits of them. All of these writers sat alone at their tables, reading their own works, their heads tilted down, their fingers turning the pages. They didn't seem to notice one another at all.

"They achieved fame but at such an awful price," Joe said softly.

I could see they were lonely and filled with regret. Hemingway, bullish and wide, was clearly cranky. Plath was pale and meek.

"Such an irony," I said.

"Alone for all time. They are famous, yes, but alone for all time. A joyless eternity."

Then I saw this southern man, John Kennedy Toole, who only became famous when he killed himself.

"I know what you're thinking, and it's wrong. His mother brought his novel to Robert Penn Warren after her son died and begged for his help."

"Toole went back?"

"Yes, he had a week to persuade anyone that he was worthy of fame. So he convinced his mother, who had never read any of his work before that. She then took his unpublished manuscript to Robert Penn Warren."

Just then, Hemingway's head opened up right where he had placed the rifle. "What's that?" I exclaimed.

"Their moment of death haunts them throughout eternity," Joe told me. "The newbie up here is David Foster Wallace. Such a sad case. He was famous, loved, and admired, yet he took his own life."

Then Plath grew green and yellow and coughed just like she must have done when she put her head in the oven. But it only lasted a few seconds. When it was over, she went back to reading her works.

I asked to see Herman Melville, and Joe took me to him. He was as stern as I'd expected and there he was on a dock. Ahab was standing beside Melville and they looked surprisingly similar. They were standing side by side in a very stiff way looking out to the ocean, and I imagined they were scanning the horizon to see if they could catch a glimpse of Moby Dick. At first I found it odd that Melville, with all his children and his long-suffering wife, had chosen Ahab, his own creation, to spend eternity with. But then I thought perhaps it made sense, as the two men clearly had a deep understanding of each other.

We went on to visit Hawthorne who sat in a pictur-esque cottage writing with a quill pen; outside his window all the characters who populated his short sto-ries and novels enjoyed quiet conversation.

———

The next-to-last place Joe took me was to the top of a very high hill. I looked down and saw thousands and thousands of writers. "Sixty thousand to be exact," Joe said. "Not one of them is famous. Not one," Joe repeated. "And every one of them on the threshold. But they truly tip the other way into total anonymity."

The thought of total facelessness, namelessness, and insignificance made me tremble. "I want to see them."

"No, you don't," Joe said.

I could see a town with sidewalks and streetlamps. I saw men and women milling around. I slowly made my way down the hill and heard Joe call to me. "Don't."

But I did and I regretted it. I saw those thousands of souls on the verge of fame and I could see the one thing they had in common. They had no faces. Not one of them. They looked up at me, probably sensing my presence. They were exactly that: faceless.

Joe reached my side. "They do not have a chance of ever being recognized. They can leave their hell but they are all too stubborn to go. They wait for the impossible to happen. Sad thing is, some of them are truly talented and some of them wrote wonderful things in their lifetimes."

There had to be several centuries of writers milling around, going all the way back to Seneca the Younger's time in ancient Rome. There were some ancient Greek playwrights whose works were burned in the Middle Ages and lost for all time; they seemed to suffer the most. They knew deep in their hearts that they would never leave this valley.

Joe could read my thoughts and he said, "The majority, however, are just arrogant and in denial."

"They have no way of ever leaving?" I asked.

"I suppose you can say it's not impossible but certainly not probable," Joe answered.

I turned away from that valley and that sad town of the insignificant.

Joe then brought me back up the hill and showed me another valley with thousands of writers milling around, lurking, walking, and just existing. Most of all, they were waiting for someone in life to discover or rediscover them. "Some of these writers actually have a chance. You would be surprised how many were down here at one time."

"Tell me," I said.

"Henry James. His books went out of print less than a year before he died. He sat down here sullen and dismayed. And he would have stayed here if a protégée of his, Edith Wharton, hadn't demanded that his books be reprinted after his famous brother and literary executor, the educator William James, made it difficult for the publisher to keep them in print. Wharton succeeded by threatening to pull her own very popular books from the publisher. And why did his brother make such trouble? Because he feared from reading Henry's letters after he died that Henry was a homosexual; he was concerned about a scandal.

"And Hart Crane was out of print until English teachers had their students start studying him in U.S. high schools. So many authors had their fortunes changed. Both ways, too." Joe stopped talking and hesitated a moment. He sighed and I understood.

"I'm destined for this valley, aren't I?"

Joe nodded. "Sorry, Tom, but yes, you are."

We descended and as we got closer to the mass of people walking around in circles, I could hear the haunting phrase, "Any news?" I first thought it was a bird chirping or a squirrel but then I realized it was human voices, hundreds and hundreds of them: "Any news?"

The strident voices rose from this valley into the surrounding hills. The phrase was repeated by men and women of all ages and from all centuries, writers who had been waiting for news from life, wondering and waiting to hear if the world had deemed them worthy. Some were popular writers of their times, like a Stephen King was to mine, and others had been studied in their own lifetimes, as James Joyce was in his.

Despite the beauty of the setting, despite the lush valley and the green rolling hills, I felt a sense of dread the closer I got to the Valley itself. My feeling of dread came from my knowing that this was where I would spend the rest of eternity if I wasn't deemed worthy of never-ending fame. The thought crushed me. I wanted to be happy ever after with my characters at my side, laughing and quoting the lines I had written.

I wondered if I had a fear of success so deeply buried in my subconscious that I had never become aware of it. Was I afraid of being famous and the demands that success makes on you? How you have to change, be available, put your work out there and embrace rejection as if it were a hug instead of a slap in the face?

I realized all that mattered now was that I had to be with the Eternals.

CHAPTER 6

Once we reached the Valley's floor I shuddered. I felt the sky close in over me.

"Relax," Joe said.

"It's claustrophobic," I told him.

"You will feel fine in a while. Accept it. Don't fight it."

I stopped. "I want to see Oscar Wilde. And I want to see Charles Bukowski."

Joe was clearly perplexed. "That means we have to go back to the Eternals."

I explained. "Please, I need to see them. They both went through tough times in life, one being imprisoned for loving another man and the other drinking while battling the insanity and deadening pain of everyday life. Wilde, dying broke and ignored, and Bukowski, becoming famous despite being drunk and ignored—I believe they could give me some words of wisdom."

Seconds later I was facing Wilde. We were outside a theater in late nineteenth-century London. There was no one else on the street, though I did hear a horse and buggy off in the distance. It was late in the day and he was dressed in black and white from head to toe. He began to walk and I walked alongside him. He was very quiet for a few steps; then he looked at me as if I were some kind of insect vying for his attention.

"I need words of wisdom from you," I said meekly. "I'm in the Valley of Those on the Verge. I don't know if I can bear it."

I waited a long time and then he said to me, "Being on the verge is like foreplay without a partner. You must learn to love yourself thoroughly." And then he walked on.

"Helpful?" Joe asked appearing behind me.

"Of course it was."

I found Charles Bukowski in a bar that had a big neon sign outside that said BUKOWSKI'S – DRINK ALL YOU WANT FOR FREE.

I walked inside and there he was, sitting on the bar. That's right, sitting in a big chair *actually* built into and atop the bar. There were all kinds of people in the bar including some important literary figures and a lot of glamorous, beautiful women.

I saw who I thought was Thornton Wilder sitting in the corner smiling and sipping a cocktail. "Are you Thornton Wilder?" I asked, stunned that he'd be in Bukowski's bar.

"Fun, isn't it?" he said. "Every once in a while I leave our town, or I should say my town, where everything is so New England, and come here to skid row to have a really amusing time," he told me. "I've escaped by the skin of my teeth some nights, ha!" He grinned.

Fitzgerald was also there sipping a martini with Zelda on his arm. "I love slumming," he muttered to no one in particular.

I walked over to Bukowski who was barefoot and unshaven. He had a big smile on his face. "Writer, huh?" he asked, but he already knew.

"Yes, Tom Chillo. I'm waiting in the Valley of Those on the Verge and I wonder if you had any advice for me."

"I don't give advice. It's a tricky proposition. You see, opinions are like assholes. Everyone has one. But on the other hand, everyone needs one." He knocked down a slug of booze.

"Okay, so how about a point of view?" I asked.

"Sure. Stick with it."

"Stick with it?"

"If you're in it for the long haul, stick with it."

I left the bar, walked into the bright sunlight of skid row, and quickly found Joe.

"It's time," he told me.

—⁓—

I slowly learned over a period of time, which of course was difficult to measure, that Wilde was right: existence in the Valley was all about loving yourself. I knew that back in life I had confused being in love with myself with being in love with my work.

I also found that those who existed here were comfortable. They weren't lacking any human needs or experiencing any earthly pains. There was no need for food or water, no need for sleep or fear of enemies or even fear of competition from other writers. The world in the Valley consisted of one beautiful day after another where you felt and looked your best (it didn't matter what you looked like when you died; in the Writers Afterlife you looked as good as you wanted to) and mostly never felt lonely, as you were surrounded by people.

At first I spent my time walking around with Joe, mingling with the others, catching glimpses of faces that all shared a distinct look of anxiety. I saw clothing from every era of humanity. Once in a while someone jumped, then beamed with joy when his or her name was called over a loudspeaker. This meant that someone on Earth, some critic or publisher, had decided this writer's work was worthy of being anthologized or produced or mentioned in an important literary newspaper or blog, or some movie production occurred and people were praising the writer. It didn't mean they were famous but it did mean someone back in life took notice of them.

Joe took me from one end of the Valley to the other and in all that time, however long it took, only a couple of writers' names had been announced; only two writers were allowed out of the Valley and into the Hall of Fame where the Eternals dwelled.

One was a Chinese writer named Su Shi, born in 1037. For some reason the present government had reprinted his books, announcing that he was the perfect *voice* for the time. His lyric poetry was now in style. I watched the dignified old man step into a bright light that nearly carried him to "the abode where the Eternal are," as Shelley wrote of Keats.

As I watched him rise into the clouds, Joe told me, "He managed to infiltrate the Chinese government and persuade them that his poetry would help them in the new century. He had been waiting a long time for a result and now all the work he had done has come to fruition."

The second writer was a Scandinavian poet. On his one-shot journey back to life, he had convinced a Norwegian university professor in Minnesota to teach his poetry; three years later in that course, a student wrote a biography of the poet for his thesis, which soon became published. In a few short years, the poet's work was once again scrutinized by the literary world and he was now thought of as one of the best poets of his generation.

The poet, looking dapper in his suit and tie, walked with a meaningful stride through the throngs of the unhappy until he reached the outer rim of the Valley. At that moment, a ray of light flew across the hill above him and guided him up into the land of the eternally famous.

"He did it," Joe said to me. "It took a hundred years, but he did it." Joe looked at me. "Sometimes it takes longer. Look at the painter Caravaggio. I knew him back in Rome. After he died, his work was considered awful because it wasn't like Michelangelo's, who'd glorified beauty. Caravaggio disliked that kind of work immensely even though he was named after the great painter—did you know that his birth name was Michelangelo Merisi? He was called the anti-painter because he painted realism. Now, five hundred years after his death, he is as popular as his namesake."

"You *knew* Caravaggio?" I asked, in awe.

Joe clearly didn't want to answer because Caravaggio was now famous and Joe was not.

Sometime in the early days of my time in the Valley of Those on the Verge, Joe took me aside and gave me the talk I was dreading. We were sitting near a pretty stream where clear water rushed over smooth rocks and birds sang and flew over our heads. We sat in the sun in a picturesque setting, feeling the gentle breeze around us.

"I will be leaving you now," Joe told me.

"Why?"

"I was your guide and now you are on your own."

I watched Joe closely. It was probably an automatic reaction when you know someone was leaving you for good. I studied his handsome face with its clear brown eyes and strong features. "What happens next?"

"Eternity," he answered.

I sat back and felt for the very first time the anxiety he had told me about. It hit me in the gut and stayed there for a few seconds, then it left and I could breathe again.

"Here are your choices. You can linger in the Valley, make friends, and find ways of enduring the fact that you weren't as talented as you thought you were. Most here accept being on the verge. Or you can make a plan to go back and try to persuade the living that you deserve perpetual fame. As I explained earlier, everyone in the Valley has that opportunity."

"If I want to do that, what does it entail?"

Joe nodded, figuring I would ask that question. "Formulate a plan. In other words, pick people you believe can change your future. Choose a handful of live people whom you can visit and try to persuade to promote your work, so that you may be rediscovered."

"Like Shakespeare, right?"

"Yes, and now I will tell you the rest of that story. The man who showed up in London one dreary night and met Jacob Tonson in a pub was Shakespeare himself. That must have had a profound effect on Jacob Tonson. Can you see it? A drunk Tonson in a pub late at night, when William Shakespeare walks through the pub doors, steps up to him, and blurts out, 'Make me famous, Jacob.' The next morning—and this is a fact—Jacob Tonson bailed Samuel Johnson out of debtors' prison and hired him to complete something Johnson had been working on for years for his publisher but had been drinking too much to complete. The work was entitled *Proposals for Printing, by Subscription, the Dramatick Works of William Shakespeare*."

"No shit?"

"Yes, my friend. It's worked more often than you'd care to believe."

I started to walk restlessly back and forth, worried that Joe would disappear before I could ask any more questions. I stopped pacing. "So, I can go back as myself?"

"Yes, or as someone else. You are allowed to create a new identity whom you *can* go back as. You give this newly invented character a backstory, a physical appearance, a reason for promoting your work. You're a writer, so it can't be too difficult. Then when you are ready and feel you have the courage, just go stand under that very large elm tree over there and say, "I'm ready.""

"I say 'I'm ready?'"

"Yes. Everything you have preplanned will be set up for you with this new identity. You will then be transported back to your world. You will have exactly one week to persuade those you have chosen to promote your work."

"One week?"

"Yes. This is heightened reality we're talking about. One week is enough time to create the workings of a drama. A movie is two hours, more or less. A play sometimes takes a little longer. Remember, no one is forcing you to do this. You have all the time in the world to decide. But if and when you do decide, you will only have one week, *one week* to do all you can. You won't need nourishment and you won't need to sleep. You will walk the earth as a living breathing human, an invention of your own imagination who can say anything to make sure that Tom Chillo, author of *The Dead Mexican*, *The Last Vision*, and eight plays, plus cowriter of four screenplays, deserves to spend eternity with other Eternals."

I nodded so many times during his talk that I thought he'd say something about my moving head, but he didn't. He kept on talking. "Remember, Arthur Rimbaud only had one book, *A Season in Hell*, to assure his fame. Rimbaud stopped writing when he turned seventeen years old and he is as famous today as he was then. You have two excellent novels. Pearl S. Buck wrote dozens of novels but only one is read today: *The Good Earth*. And she's famous. Do you want to see her?"

"No. She shouldn't be famous," I said.

"Of course not. But that should egg you on. She's famous, why aren't you?"

I nodded my head in agreement.

"Do what you can. Fight your bad luck. Create your own destiny," he said. "You plan it out. You have imagination. Just keep in mind, as I told you before, that so many became famous this way."

I stopped nodding my head.

"Any more questions?" he asked. "You have lots."

"So I have to find a few people or at least one person who can actually make me famous even though I'm dead, even though I won't write another thing, even though I can't speak for myself?"

"Yes."

"Then my choices are either to accept existence in the Valley of Those on the Verge for all time or to go back to life for one week and change my destiny so I can rid myself of this awful anxiety of never being thought of as a great writer?"

"That's it in a nutshell," Joe said. But then he took a breath and said, "There's one last thing."

"Really? What?"

"You can leave the Valley."

"There's another place to go?"

"You can leave The Writers Afterlife and join the others."

"What others?"

Joe sat back on his elbow. "The normal ones. The ordinary people. The rest of humanity and wherever it is *they* dwell after they die. But if you leave, you can never come back to the Writers Afterlife. If you decide you didn't have enough talent to live anywhere in the Writers Afterlife, either in the Valley or with the Eternals, you can never return and even if you become famous, you won't ever learn that fact."

"Do some of these people do that?" I asked, gesturing to the wandering hopefuls who filled the Valley.

"Oh yes, more than you'd think. Every day more and more leave. It takes some a few centuries to give up and some give up after just a few years. Existing in the Valley is an awful fate sometimes," Joe told me.

As befitting any parting of the ways, the sun began to set as I walked with Joe to the end of the Valley.

"I hope you gain what you need to make you eternally happy. And if you don't, I hope you learn to accept your providence," he told me, and then he was gone.

Joe had left my sight as if he was a flicker of light, a moment in time, a fleeting memory.

CHAPTER 7

Her name was Jennifer. She had begun publishing in the 1970s and wound up writing four novels, a book of short stories, and two volumes of poetry. She had published with a major publisher as well as some small presses that had begun emerging in that decade. Jennifer was Eurasian and had taught at Vassar as an adjunct. She'd married but never had any children. She was delicate-looking with long dark brown hair and large brown eyes. She had an actress's features: button nose, sensual lips, and dimples in her cheeks. She didn't consider herself a feminist but she'd lived the life, the real life of a woman writer.

We spent a lot of time talking. I wasn't sure when or where I had met her, as time in the Writers Afterlife had no fixed definition. All I could recall was that one day I was walking in a field and she was walking beside me. We found a blanket on a hill just waiting for us so we sat down in the warm sun and talked. As I said, we might have talked for months or weeks or only hours. Time on Earth moved so differently it was hard to make that distinction.

Like me, Jennifer was waiting to decide on what course to take, planning her one chance to go back and whom to see when she did. Like me, she'd died in her forties, but as she'd died in 1998, she'd been waiting longer. She was more productive than I'd been, though she hadn't written any screenplays.

She said I looked handsome and in my twenties; to me she looked pretty and in her early twenties. It was amazing how our imaginations had such power in the Writers Afterlife.

"I'm afraid to go back," she told me eventually.

"Why?" I asked.

"I met so many who did go back and still haven't heard a thing. Some of them have been waiting for more than a few centuries. See that woman over there? She wrote a book of poems. She knew Elizabeth Barrett Browning. She went back right after she died, and nothing!"

I saw a young woman sitting under a tree. Her face was hidden by shadows. Only her legs and lap were lit by the bright sunlight.

"She has been sitting there ever since I first met her."

"What's her name?" I asked.

"Does it matter?" Jennifer replied, terrified as if she were speaking about herself.

After that we walked for a few hours or days. There was no sign of time passing. The sun was always shining, the landscape green, and the sky blue. If we decided to find a café, we were instantly sitting in one. We talked about our favorite writers and movies and of course, I knew more than she did since there were so many published books and movies made since she died. I enjoyed talking with her. Her voice was so warm and friendly, her eyes so pretty, and her smile so inviting.

I could tell she enjoyed me as well because she never stopped looking at me. She laughed a lot at some of the silly things I said, and I laughed at her determination and how serious she was sometimes about everything.

"I don't even think of Mark," she told me.

"Your husband?"

"Yes. We were married right after we both graduated from Columbia. But I never think of him. I heard he remarried and I say, 'Okay, good for him.' I feel no sense of loss or regret about my life with him."

"Did he love you?"

"Oh yes, more than I deserved. He gave up having children with me and he slowed down the pursuit of his own career as a filmmaker just to stay in New York and live with me."

"How did you die?"

Jennifer smirked. "So stupidly. A car crash."

"Wow," I said.

Jennifer lowered her voice. "I was drunk."

I leaned in closer.

"I was an alcoholic, you know."

She told me this with the cold eye of an objective narrator. "One night I was driving in the rain on the FDR Drive and I was angry because I'd just had a new novel rejected by Simon & Schuster and I hit a wall. Just hit a wall. No seatbelt. My skull cracked. My spine was split.

"Mark cried like a baby at my wake. My father was devastated. I was his perfect little girl. My mother, also an alcoholic, just stared at me in the coffin."

"And it all flew by like a movie," I said.

"Yes, it did. My family was Catholic so I had the priest and the wake and the funeral and the burial. So quickly it all went," she agreed.

We sat in silence for a few moments. "Are you going back soon?" she asked.

"I've been thinking a lot about picking the right time and the right people to meet. I have also been thinking of the right person to be when I go back. I have to create someone with purpose. Timing is everything with a plan like this, but you also have to persuade someone who can make a difference. To answer your question, I'm not sure yet."

"But you will go soon?"

I nodded. "Yes. However, there's another thing about going back that I haven't figured out yet. I've been thinking about something that I need to work out. When I figure that out, I will go."

Jennifer moved a little to her right. She had one hand on her leg and the other was folded underneath her. "I thought I'd go to my editor. I thought then perhaps my publisher and my agent."

"Good choices."

"But how do I persuade them that my work is good enough to be great? What do I tell them to help them see that?" she asked.

"Do you believe you are a great writer?"

"Yes," she said quickly.

"Truly?"

"Don't test me," she shot back.

"But it is a test, Jen. They are testing you. They need to know that you are passionate about being worthy. They want to see that passion in action. They want to see you change fate. Do you know how difficult it is to change your own destiny? But the greats did just that. They lived way beyond human boundaries when it came to making sure their names were expansive and flowed without resistance through all time."

Jennifer seemed stunned by my sudden outburst. Then she said sweetly, "Help me."

I shuddered when she did. Why? Because I wanted to help her, and that impulse to help another writer was dangerous. I knew that to go out of my way to help someone else was wrong especially when I should be focusing on my own immortality.

Up to that point I was pretty sure that there was no chance of having romantic feelings in the Writers Afterlife but I was having them and it was confusing. I wasn't sure if it was a test or not. Was my dedication to eternal renown being put under some kind of very intense scrutiny? Or did the human desire for love and romance exist in this afterlife?

Jennifer leaned toward me, took my hand, and looked up at me. I could see sincere concern in her eyes. "I'm not wired for this kind of thing," she said. "Mark wanted to have children, but I couldn't focus on loving anything but my writing. He wanted my love, and I could only give him my body for sex and my attention when he really needed it. I felt like a freak my whole life, Tom. A freak of nature."

"You were and still are an artist. An author to be exact. That's how we are. We fail as human beings and we are exceptional at understanding human nature. Most of us are just more comfortable around fiction than real life."

Soon we found ourselves walking along a large lake that spread its waters west into the setting sun. It was glorious and expansive and it made us walk closer. She took my hand in hers. Or did I reach for her hand first? I wasn't sure.

"Who are you going to be when you go back?" she asked.

I didn't want to tell her. I wondered if she'd steal my idea because that's what it was, really—an idea. One I couldn't copyright, however. "*You* should go back as an Internet publisher of e-books, perhaps on Amazon, who wants to reprint Jennifer's novels and short stories," I said.

"That's a good idea," she told me.

"You should look for the executor of your work. Your literary executor."

"That's Mark."

I frowned.

She noticed. "I know. I worry that he resented me so much during our time together he would just drop the ball. His new wife has no career at all. They just had a child."

"You must see him and this new woman and persuade him to get someone else to act as executor."

Jennifer nodded.

"There has to be someone who loved your work without any jealousy. Someone who sincerely liked your writing and felt no sense of competition. It happens, though rarely. Even normal people become envious of us. Was there anyone?" I asked.

Jennifer nodded again. "Sue. Sue was my best friend. She's such a lonely woman. Never married. Not very attractive. She lived vicariously through me."

"Great! Get Mark to appoint *her* as the literary executrix of your estate. Go see her as this new woman. Or go back as a gorgeous blonde from California or the Midwest. Someone so different from you. Show them the wide appeal your work has. Make this woman a lesbian singly focused on advancing women's literature."

eyes, and her neck. I heard her moan and
shoulders. She pulled me closer, rubbing her
er my arms, across my stomach, and on my
e wanted to feel how masculine I was, she
experience the virility she once knew when
ive.

n't fall in love," I told her. "Neither of us is
it."

ust thinking that. I could never love you. But I
," she told me.

s all we can afford here. Needing has a price
as expensive as loving," I said.

e moon, white and cold, darting in and out of
s. I heard her breathing and I could nearly
eart.

her ear to my chest. She wanted to listen to
as I was listening to hers. "Impossible," she

h here is impossible," I agreed.

stop me, Tom. Please, don't stop me from
vhat I was born for," she said.

exactly what she meant. I knew exactly how
was as much her as she was me. We were
ame alien species of a subdivision of human
had the same DNA messages programming

I was on a roll of inspiration, moving along at the
speed of light, and Jennifer was taking it all in.

"When should I go back?" she asked.

I knew she wasn't ready so I wanted her to go now. I
wanted her to fail. I was falling in love with her and yet I
wanted her to bomb to make sure that there was room
for me and my work on the shelf of the immortal writers.
I felt a pang of anxiety just thinking that she might
become more famous than me.

"Now?" she asked, pushing me for an answer.

I shook my head. "Not now. You're not ready." It felt
so strange to tell the truth, to choose her over me.

She hugged me. Right there in the broad daylight, she
hugged me. "That's for being truthful. You're right. I'm
not ready." Suddenly it was twilight and we were standing
under a tree and kissing in the shadows.

I was quickly lost in the sensuality of her lips. I felt
myself pressing against her. I took her head in my hands
and gently moved her closer. I felt her tongue. It was
moist and I wanted more. I put my hand on her hips and
I felt her react. She edged her body closer to mine. She
put her hand on my hips, feeling for my thigh. And then
it all stopped. Jennifer pulled away and disappeared.

I looked for her all night. It was a night I had created
with my own fears. I was startled. I wanted to ask Joe

how I had emotions and fears when I wasn't supposed to
have them. And then I realized he had lied to me. His
job was to lie to me. I was going to have fears and anxiety and loneliness and desires for the rest of eternity as
long as I lived in the Valley of Those on the Verge.

CHA

'm not sure how mu
Jennifer again. She wa
of her novels. I walked
"This is wrong for bot
you?" she said, looking up
"They lied to us."
"Yes, they did."
"We are as human here
"Only as long as we are
I found myself holding
were. Then I looked up
bed, in an apartment, in
that lined the world outs
and we were both nake

face, he
touch n
fingers
thighs.
needed
she was
"We
capable
"I wa
do *need*
"Nee
but it's
I saw
thin clo
hear he
She
my hea
told me
"So
"Do
achievi
I kn
she felt
from th
being.

us. We shared everything, right down to the molecules that made us. We were driven by the same obsession.

"Do you really exist?" she asked, touching my hand as she did.

"I know I do. But do you?" I asked.

"I'm flesh and blood, Tom. Well, I was once."

Neither of us moved. I knew that in the Writers Afterlife the imagination was everything, so it was very possible that I had created Jennifer out of my own need. It was also very likely that if she actually did exist in this timeless land, she had imagined me.

"Kiss me," she said.

I did. The kiss lasted perhaps hours or just seconds. When I gently pulled my lips away from her, she was no longer there. I had eradicated her and at the same time she had eradicated me. It had to be that way if we were to concentrate on our goal.

Though she was gone, I could smell her scent for what seemed like months. I could remember how her body felt in my arms as if I had held her for years. She was with me everywhere I went in the Valley, but I refused to see her and I knew in what remained of my heart that she refused to see me.

Time passed. I was now lonelier than ever before. I wanted to be with Jennifer but I also wanted to complete my soul and find a home in eternity for it. I needed to make Tom Chillo as great a name as Melville and Geoffrey Chaucer.

I roamed the rocky hills under the gray clouds like a madman unable to stop. I thought hard about my plan of whom to see when I went back to life.

I thought about Sarah and how I needed to remove her from being my executrix. She loved me but what remained of me, my books, she didn't love and she wasn't doing anything for my immortality. Claudia was different. She had something to benefit from my success after death because she'd been my agent and she could still market my work and profit from it. I also knew that she adored my writing ever since she discovered me when I first got my Masters from Columbia. She saved me from oblivion when she managed to get Simon & Schuster to publish *The Dead Mexican*.

I also planned on seeing Doug Harris, the blogging literary critic who had given me wonderful reviews. I was formulating a plan; it was slowly coming together. I thought I'd return exactly a year after my death—in real-life time, the one-year anniversary of my death.

Eventually, I stopped roaming around and went into a bar. I needed to be in a dark place where everything was made of wood and looked sturdy and where I could lean and think. So I created what I needed and met Jack.

In his fifties, he was burly and yet still youthful. He had

I was on a roll of inspiration, moving along at the speed of light, and Jennifer was taking it all in.

"When should I go back?" she asked.

I knew she wasn't ready so I wanted her to go now. I wanted her to fail. I was falling in love with her and yet I wanted her to bomb to make sure that there was room for me and my work on the shelf of the immortal writers. I felt a pang of anxiety just thinking that she might become more famous than me.

"Now?" she asked, pushing me for an answer.

I shook my head. "Not now. You're not ready." It felt so strange to tell the truth, to choose her over me.

She hugged me. Right there in the broad daylight, she hugged me. "That's for being truthful. You're right. I'm not ready." Suddenly it was twilight and we were standing under a tree and kissing in the shadows.

I was quickly lost in the sensuality of her lips. I felt myself pressing against her. I took her head in my hands and gently moved her closer. I felt her tongue. It was moist and I wanted more. I put my hand on her hips and I felt her react. She edged her body closer to mine. She put her hand on my hips, feeling for my thigh. And then it all stopped. Jennifer pulled away and disappeared.

I looked for her all night. It was a night I had created with my own fears. I was startled. I wanted to ask Joe how I had emotions and fears when I wasn't supposed to have them. And then I realized he had lied to me. His job was to lie to me. I was going to have fears and anxiety and loneliness and desires for the rest of eternity as long as I lived in the Valley of Those on the Verge.

face, her eyes, and her neck. I heard her moan and touch my shoulders. She pulled me closer, rubbing her fingers over my arms, across my stomach, and on my thighs. She wanted to feel how masculine I was, she needed to experience the virility she once knew when she was alive.

"We can't fall in love," I told her. "Neither of us is capable of it."

"I was just thinking that. I could never love you. But I do *need* you," she told me.

"Need is all we can afford here. Needing has a price but it's not as expensive as loving," I said.

I saw the moon, white and cold, darting in and out of thin clouds. I heard her breathing and I could nearly hear her heart.

She put her ear to my chest. She wanted to listen to my heart as I was listening to hers. "Impossible," she told me.

"So much here is impossible," I agreed.

"Don't stop me, Tom. Please, don't stop me from achieving what I was born for," she said.

I knew exactly what she meant. I knew exactly how she felt. I was as much her as she was me. We were from the same alien species of a subdivision of human being. We had the same DNA messages programming

CHAPTER 8

I'm not sure how much time passed before I saw Jennifer again. She was sitting at a table reading one of her novels. I walked over to her.

"This is wrong for both of us; you know that, don't you?" she said, looking up.

"They lied to us."

"Yes, they did."

"We are as human here as we were back on Earth."

"Only as long as we are *here*, in the Valley," she said.

I found myself holding her. I wasn't sure where we were. Then I looked up and I saw that we were in a bed, in an apartment, in a building with lit windows that lined the world outside the window. It was night and we were both naked. I held her and kissed her written four Broadway plays. He knew William Inge; he'd been with him the day before he committed suicide. Inge was on the verge even though so many thought he should be an Eternal. I didn't see him in the Valley. I heard that he'd committed suicide not to be famous but because he was depressed that he had lost his fame while still alive. There were so many like Inge haunting the hills and trees.

"I hate these boundaries!" Jack would pontificate. He was a barrel of a man with thin strands of hair, shoulders like mountains, and small, dark blue eyes that could see in the dark. "I hate, and hate keeps me here."

"You went back early on?" I asked.

"Yes. I was sure it was the best thing to do. I spent the week just as they had said I should. I knew exactly who I had to see. I saw a celebrated producer. He took all my plays to Broadway. But when I saw him again all he did was bad-mouth my plays, calling me second-rate. He made a fortune on my work but to him I was nothing more than a meal ticket."

We were suddenly leaning on a bar rail in an exclusive club. I was being eyed by a startling blond cigarette girl. But I wasn't there for her; I was there to learn from Jack and his mistakes.

"My wife got all my royalties. She was a slut from the day I met her but the problem was I always liked sluts. I didn't mind that, it was just that she didn't care about my work. I also had a son who joined the army. He hated my being a writer. He thought it was an embarrassing career. He wanted me to be a general."

"So, who did you see?

"The person you should never see. I went to my best friend. He directed all my plays."

"And?"

"In one meeting, in one sit-down in a coffee shop on Broadway, in less than a half an hour, I learned that all those years he was directing my plays, he never forgave me for being more talented than he was."

I watched Jack slug down his scotch and water.

"Bob buried my plays. Once I died he never directed another play of mine. He refused to direct revivals, no matter how big a star wanted to be in it," Jack said, and then turned to me. "That director single-handedly buried my career as good as if he burned everything I had ever written."

"Wow," I said. "What did you do?"

"When I realized how much he hated me, I killed him."

I smirked. "You couldn't kill him. You're dead. You were playing a part."

"I pushed him off the pier on the Lower East Side. Say I didn't kill him all you want. I saw him in the river and I know he never came up for air."

I looked around and whispered, "Did they punish you?"

It was now Jack's turn to smirk. "I'm here in the Valley talking to you, aren't I? That's punishment enough." He lowered his head for a moment then looked up into the neon lights that showed their blurry existence outside the window. "If you got the guts to go back, control your temper when you do."

I was dumbfounded but asked another question. "Did you go back as yourself?"

"I went back as myself but younger, so I wasn't recognized at first," he answered. He then slugged down the rest of his drink. "There are more acting schools and actors in New York City now then there are cockroaches and they never do scenes from my plays. Never!"

At that point, I decided to leave. I figured I'd met him because he was a lesson. Larger than life, determined to be famous, and in the end, all he could do was commit manslaughter in the name of immortality.

As I wandered away he shouted a warning at me: "Beware the spirit of resentment."

I stopped.

Jack looked intently at me. "There are those who will appear in your life when you go back to life. Some of them will be flesh and blood and others will be apparitions sent back to life by other writers jealous of you."

"Is that possible?" I asked.

Jack nodded. "They won't tell you who sent them. They didn't even tell you that anyone could. But there are those who will stop at nothing to keep you from being immortal. They will even give up their own one chance of going back to stop you from walking up that hill!" He pointed to where the Eternals dwelled and I knew right then that there was more to this Writers Afterlife than Joe had explained.

I left the bar and walked a few hours, allowing the urban winds to blow me wherever they wanted. I watched paper cups and garbage fly by through alleys and scamper over sidewalks. I heard a blues band playing in a small club and the sad moan of a saxophone calmed me, but only for a few moments until I realized that I was still in the Valley of Those on the Verge and still had to come up with some plan to change my destiny.

My guide, Joe, never made it clear to me that the particular suffering I was going to endure in the Valley was just like the suffering I had endured in life. It was the suffering of never truly being famous. He also left out another big essential difference. In life some people, not writers but ordinary people, were usually sympathetic to your plight, but in the Valley all you met were other writers who also suffered from the same affliction and had no sympathy for you at all. Hence, your suffering in this afterlife was worse because you knew it might last for all time.

One day I needed to find some relief from my suffering and walked to the top of the hill where Goethe lived but I was stopped by a uniformed cop in NYPD blue before I reached Goethe's front door. "You can't be here. You're restricted," the cop said to me.

"Restricted?"

"You're not allowed to mingle with the greats," he said.

I felt humiliated. "Who are you, by the way, that they let you up here?" I asked.

"I'm Timmy Nolan. I was a cop back in life. I wrote a novel, though. Maybe you heard of it: *Blue Badge*. Anyway, I got shot in the head and killed during a drug bust gone wrong. I was sent to the Writers Afterlife," he told me.

Now I remembered him and his book. "They made a TV series out of your novel," I said.

He smiled, clearly enjoying my being aware of him. "That's right."

"And you're here waiting to be famous?"

"Why not?" He looked annoyed. "Other cops who wrote books are up here. Do you have something against cop writers?"

"Actually, I do. I also have a problem with lawyer writers and doctor writers."

"Turn around and head back down the hill before I cuff you and take you down to the precinct for disturbing the peace," he said roughly.

"What precinct?" I asked.

"The one in my imagination, pal," he answered. "You're not the only writer here."

I walked down the hill toward the ocean and the night. I stayed on the beach all night hoping to lose myself in the night sky. That was when I realized that hope was all I had left. I realized it was time I went back to life.

I went to the very tall elm tree that Joe had pointed out to me. "I'm ready," I pronounced as Joe told me to.

But I had a request *within* my request. I asked if my week back to life could be divided in half so that I would return to life on a Sunday morning and be back in the Afterlife by Wednesday at midnight. I could then return for a final time from Thursday morning to Sunday by dawn a year later. I thought the extra time would give the ability to access the impact I would have on those I visited and come up with a change in strategy if need be.

My request was quickly accepted. I knew this because I just did. No one told me, it was just clear.

CHAPTER 9

I made my first appearance in post-death life by standing at the East River right above the FDR Drive on a day in late May only a block away from the Fourteenth Street entrance. It was 6:20 a.m. and the sun was slowly rising over Queens.

I watched the sunlight brighten the steel and metal cable structure of the Brooklyn Bridge to my right. I watched the surface of the East River go from murky gray to a cool blue as the sunlight shone across it. The sun slowly covered my face with an orange glow, and I watched the darkness retreat from the growing light as the sky grew a lighter and lighter blue until it gently transformed into true-blueness.

I picked a new name, Max Foreman, and I was staying at the Tribeca Grand Hotel where it seems I had reserved a room. I was publisher of a small press called Northern Books in Toronto and I wanted to publish an anthology of Tom Chillo's fiction. As Max Foreman, I was in New York to accomplish several things. First, I needed the rights to his work so I could publish them; and second, I needed someone of respected literary reputation to write a foreword to the anthology.

I made Max in his early thirties, with an engaging smile. He was six foot three with open, warm blue eyes and combed-back rich black hair. Max was clean-shaven and had an easygoing personality, possessing a quiet charm. He was intelligent and modest about his looks. I gave him a sturdy yet soft voice. He was deliberate, concise and low-key. I made him everything Tom Chillo wasn't. Tom Chillo was nervous, energetic, and said too much, thought too much, felt too exclusively about himself, and punished himself for working excessively, then felt guilty when he didn't write enough.

Max Foreman was free of any discernible neurosis. The only thing he had in common with Tom Chillo was that neither man ever doubted Tom Chillo was a great writer.

Several weeks before leaving the Afterlife, I sent out e-mails to set up meetings. Of the several people I'd chosen to meet with, Sarah was my first choice. She was my longtime friend, lover, helpful editor, confidante, and executrix of my work.

As our relationship grew longer and her tiny apartment grew smaller, Sarah grew older and spoke more about her childhood.

"I want room. No, I want *rooms*! Rooms upstairs and downstairs like when I was growing up. My parents owned a house. I'm almost forty, and I barely have enough room for anything!" she'd remind me most nights.

I had e-mailed her to meet me that Sunday night and she had agreed, as she was busy editing at her magazine job during the beginning of the week.

I also contacted Doug Harris. He was only thirty years old and making a name for himself on a blog that reviewed and commented on American fiction. He had grown up in England, which gave his pompous servings of literary opinion more weight to those who read him, though if you gave him a Brooklyn accent, nothing he wrote sounded articulate. He also had agreed to see me; I would take him to lunch on Monday.

I also felt very strongly about seeing my agent. Claudia was my ace in the hole. She was forty-five or so, still as lovely as a young woman. She was divorced without children, tall, slender with light-green eyes and short blond hair. She worked for William Morris Endeavor and everything about her was perfect for my plan. She loved me and my work, and even though she hadn't come to my wake, I knew she had to be overwhelmed with grief when I died.

———

Max had offered to take Sarah to brunch, so that's where I found myself: poolside at Soho House.

I was already sitting when Sarah showed up. She was lovely in a soft brown skirt and beige blouse. Her smile was miniature in scope but warm while being directed at me; her eyes were hazel and oval-shaped, revealing that she was a little self-conscious, a little shy, and mostly fretful about all things out of her control. I could see Sarah react when she saw how handsome I was—as Max, that is.

I ordered her a Bloody Mary and she accepted it. In fact, while waiting for her I had already ordered food for us. We both had Eggs Benedict and fresh fruit and coffee, and she liked that I had ordered ahead of time.

"I love Eggs Benedict," she said.

Naturally, I didn't tell her I already knew that.

"So, you want to publish an anthology of Tom's fiction?" she asked.

"I do, in a double-book set," I told her, enjoying the sound of Max's voice. It was confident but it was also reassuring.

"Why?" she asked.

I was taken aback by her asking that question. "What do you mean?"

Sarah sipped her Bloody Mary and then looked at me with strong intent. She *was* a loner. It was funny how I hadn't paid attention to that quality earlier. A loner is someone who, like it or not, spends more time alone than with other people. Loners like to look into the eyes of those they are speaking to. It makes them feel less alone.

Sarah was never sought out by her friends and I never understood why, but I was so obsessed with myself it hardly mattered to me when I was living. I did recall that many of her friends got married and moved out of the city to have children and those who stayed in the city to bring up their kids stopped calling her. Her friends who hadn't married didn't want to hang out with her because she reminded them of their own plight: the unmarried professional woman. It was all so complicated for me to understand back then.

Those were my thoughts when Sarah asked, "Why do you want to publish Tom's work?"

Before I answered I saw again that Sarah was a true loner. It was right there in the overwhelming magnitude and aura of her loneliness. Sarah was a woman who ate most of her meals alone, slept alone, woke up alone, and traveled alone. Though she knew how to do it, she had yet to accept it.

She was a soldier of the modern world where emotions were siphoned away by cell phones, iPods, and other technologies, where sadness wasn't measured by the time you spent being by yourself—it was measured against the all-American notion of family, even though that notion only truly existed in the collective imagination as a fantasy, not as an experience.

Sarah struck me as someone always in mid-conversation, midlife crisis, midair hoping to be caught, hoping to find a place to land, hoping to make sense out of anything, even to find some meaning out of the loneliness of the night before. While being Max, I was more interested in her and her plight than I had been as Tom.

"I find his work memorable and worthy to keep alive," I said, "I want to see it in print. I believe it needs much attention," I continued as Max the publisher. "The two novels were published five years apart. I know both of them could've sold better if the publishers had given them any kind of publicity. Tom never went on a book tour and he was never given a chance to do book signings. Best-selling novelists got all the attention, but critics did love his books and thanks to the Internet, several websites were created that favored his books. In fact, I learned about his work from one of those best-fiction websites. He received five stars on Amazon for both titles. The audience reviews were always raves. I even wrote one myself."

"That is all true. Wow, you certainly know about Tom."

"I want you to see my enthusiasm firsthand, because you are his literary executrix," I told her. I took a deep breath, focusing on my task. "By the way, do you have plans as his literary executrix?"

"Plans?"

"To make his work known. To get it in anthologies. To see if he can be taught in some classes. To try to sell the movie rights. That sort of thing."

"No."

"So, you are just going to collect his royalties?" I asked.

"They aren't much. But they do help pay for his father's boarding expenses in the nursing home," she replied. "I don't take anything. I never took anything from Tom."

I heard the resentment in her voice and now I knew for sure that I had to wrestle the power of literary executrix of my work out of her hands. Otherwise, unconsciously or not, she would do everything possible to bury my writing in the dust bowl of the forgotten.

She smiled at me, at Max, that is. I could tell that Sarah was affected by Max's handsomeness and she asked a lot of questions about him and his background, plans, and if he was married or not. I spent most of the brunch making stuff up to appease her curiosity.

I could see she was enjoying herself when she ordered another Bloody Mary. "Are you seeing anyone?" she asked.

"No, too busy with starting the new publishing house," I told her.

She told me how she liked the design of my website and thought Northern Books had a chance to make it. I knew all her small talk was about getting to know me and wanting me to get to know her. I told her that Tom's collection was my first foray into the publishing world and that I had made a lot of money in high-tech software a decade earlier. She smiled at me a lot and I smiled back but I kept my smiles as friendly and asexual as possible.

After brunch we walked through the Meatpacking District while the sun was still bright though descending in the western sky. I listened to Sarah, realizing I had never heard her talk so much about herself before. Not even on our first date all those years ago did she talk about herself as she was now. She was a little drunk and that made her open and vulnerable, I thought, something I hadn't seen before. Or maybe I hadn't seen it before because I never had paid attention.

"I have to get up early tomorrow," she repeated as if it was a mantra, a code for giving me the okay to invite myself up to her apartment. I, Max, had no interest in her in that way and I, Tom, felt bad for her that Max didn't. We kept walking as she talked about her life and watched cars fly by on Hudson Street with the Hudson River dark and mysterious only blocks away.

"I'm having lunch with Doug Harris tomorrow. Do you know him?"

"I know *who* he is," she answered.

"I am going to ask him to write the foreword for the double-set volume," I said.

"Did you get the rights from Simon & Schuster?" she asked. Then she quickly said, "Of course you must have gotten the rights."

I nodded and replied, "Of course I took care of that." Simon & Schuster had already replied to my letter I'd sent from the Afterlife that it was okay for me to publish his books since they were going to be out of print soon. My one big fear, any novelist's big fear: his or her books going out of print. I was hoping that print on demand would change that but it hadn't yet.

"Why Doug Harris? I don't think Tom ever spoke about knowing him."

"He gave both of Tom's novels great reviews," I said. "You must have known that." I made sure the last sentence was said as a jab, a zinger, making a point.

We turned up Sarah's street. "I'd like to be there when you talk with Doug Harris," she said looking up at me.

That was not going to happen. I needed to isolate each of those who could help me. Having them in the same room was not a good idea. "I don't think that will work out, but maybe we can have dinner on Tuesday if you are free?" I asked.

She leapt at my offer. "Yes, I can do that." She smiled as he stood outside her apartment on a tree-lined street where I had spent so many hours of my life.

"Why did we meet? For some reason I can't remember if we had a specific reason," she said tipsily.

"Tom. I wanted to know if it was okay with you, his executrix, for me to publish his two novels."

"We were lovers. But I imagine you know that." She ignored my discussion about Tom's work and quickly spoke about Tom himself and his relationship with her.

"I knew that," I said. "You were lovers for many years. He dedicated both books to you."

She lowered her head as if that really didn't matter and was not the point.

"*Friends* more than lovers, I think, now that he's gone."

"It's important having a friend," I told her. "He was a great writer," I stated, doing all I could not to sound pathetic and self-interested. I forgot that Max could never sound like that but that Tom could and *always did* sound like that.

"Do you think so?"

"Yes."

"Funny how Tom never mentioned you," she repeated. Then she changed the subject to me. "Tuesday is great. Where?"

"I'll e-mail you where."

"I never thought of Tom as a great writer or a not-so-great writer. He was Tom to me. And I loved him."

"And he loved you."

"I don't think he did, actually."

I watched Sarah enter her building and then I turned away.

I thought of her getting inside her place and how she'd put on the light. Her apartment, which had been shrinking to her, was filled with printed-out articles from *Arts & Letters Daily* and magazines including *The New York Times Book Review* section. She loved to read and then keep everything she read, as if by keeping it in her apartment she was storing it in her brain. She loved to look up references as if her inner life was a library. I'd been quite fond of that trait.

CHAPTER 10

I spent Sunday night in my room at the Tribeca Grand online searching for stories on Tom Chillo. There was an announcement of his death on the Writers Guild of America, East's website, and an Authors Guild newsletter, but that was all. So I decided to take a walk through the city.

I found myself sitting on a bench in Chelsea. I saw the dim lights from New Jersey across the Hudson River. For some reason, I didn't know why, I imagined a moment from my childhood. It was a memory from a long-distant world, a memory of mine and no one else's.

We were sitting at the dinner table in our house in Queens. The table was in the kitchen and it was only my father, my mother, and I. I was sixteen years old and my body was slowly slimming down, becoming lanky, and I was, in many ways, finding out who I was.

"I want to be a writer," I told my mother and father.

My mother stopped eating and looked at my father but she didn't say anything.

"I wanted to go to the moon when I was your age. That's just a dream, Tom. You don't live dreams. You need to go to law school and become a lawyer," my father stated.

I watched my father go back to his dinner but my mother's eyes were still trained on me. "Don't stop," she told him.

"I wanted to buy a car and drive across the country when I graduated from high school. I wanted to write what I experienced, you know, maybe become a poet," my father continued.

"You *heard* your father," my mother said.

"If he wanted to go to the moon, he should have. They did go eventually. Men did go to the moon. It's not impossible. Nothing is impossible," I replied to both of them.

My father seemed momentarily sympathetic. My mother wasn't. She put her fork down. "You're going to be one of those, aren't you?"

"One of those *who*?" I asked. For the first time in my short life I felt empowered. Just announcing something tangible about my life, telling those closest to me that I had a "calling," a vocation, gave me a confidence I didn't have before.

"You are going to be one of those who grow up to disappoint. You are going to be one of those who disappoint everyone around them." My mother's words were cruel and she meant them to be so.

"He'll change. He's young still," my father said.

My mother looked at me as if she knew that wasn't going to happen. She saw the fire in my eyes. She saw that I had changed and that I had been thinking of being a writer for a long time, longer than she, my own mother, was aware of.

"God help us," she muttered then got up from the table.

I looked at my father but he also had had enough of the conversation. I knew I had won. I had announced to my parents that I was aware that I had a gift and now I had to explore it with my fullest and most intense attention.

It was also when I realized I was an orphan. I had nothing in common with my parents. I wanted to have a life that I could reflect upon; otherwise, it wasn't worth living. My parents seemed to see me as an aberration, a mistake and not part of their DNA. I had to accept that and in doing so, it made me stronger to complete what I had set out to do: dedicate my life to writing.

The memory soon faded and so did I. I was really only a ghost and ghosts don't have memories, or so I thought. I got up from the bench and turned to walk downtown, keeping the Hudson to my right as long as I could. I needed the river to remind me that the earth was still real and that I had a mission to complete.

—∿—

Doug Harris was wiry and short but he spoke as if every word made him money and every thought he had needed to be expressed the second he had it. He had tiny eyes, a three-day beard, cropped reddish-brown hair, and wore a yellow long-sleeved shirt, black chinos, black socks and brown loafers. Looking closely at him I was sure he did something to his eyebrows, like perhaps darken them, and I was sure that he had put on eyeliner to highlight his very light blue eyes.

He also wiggled a lot when he spoke as if driven by an internal engine. When he spoke his hips moved and then a leg and sometimes his shoulder would rise up and then curve down. I quickly became exhausted listening to him.

He had his assistant, Danni, with him. Danni was petite and quite overloaded with a bag of books, her computer, and everything Doug didn't want to carry.

She had blond hair pulled tightly back and small blue eyes that stared at me during our lunch at French Roast on Sixth Avenue and Eleventh Street.

She had her Kindle on the table and was reading something as we spoke; she was also constantly checking references that came up in our conversation on her smartphone.

"What you reading?" I asked politely.

"*Ask the Dust*. This John Fante is pretty good," she answered.

I had just seen him in the Writers Afterlife but of course I didn't tell her that.

Doug Harris was the type of thirty-year-old male in the media industry who believed he had the ability to size anyone up in minutes. He believed this because he truly felt that he was the most interesting person in the room when he was in the room.

He also believed that what he didn't see didn't exist, and this belief fueled his runaway ego. Because Max was pleasant and amenable, Doug had figured he knew all he needed to know by the time it took him to take two sips of his cocktail. Of course, what Doug didn't know was that Max didn't actually exist.

"So you will pay for this foreword I'm going to write for you," Doug said quickly.

I could tell that despite Doug's massive self-importance, Max physically intimidated him. I replied that yes, I would pay for the foreword, advertise it, and be eternally grateful that Doug Harris was taking the time to do this for me. In turn, I wanted Doug to plug the book on his blog, set up some readings at the Barnes & Noble in Manhattan, NPR, and any cable TV shows and book review websites Doug had connections to.

Of course, the promise of payment would be difficult to fulfill, as I was dead. However, when I'd died there was some money in my savings account. I'd have to get Sarah to send it to Doug.

Doug lectured Danni and me on the merits of his blog as he devoured his vegetable wrap and scotch and water. Danni nipped at her salad and I easily refrained from eating anything, though I did order a tea with lemon.

"When can I see what you write?" I asked.

"As soon as I see a check," Doug said.

"You do admire Tom Chillo's work?" I asked a little too nervously.

Doug didn't miss a beat. "Excellent writer. Of course not nearly as interesting as David Foster Wallace but more interesting than that bore Jonathan Franzen."

"What is it that you admire?" I asked.

Doug looked at me. "You're publishing his books. I should be asking you that," he replied.

I was glad he didn't ask me. Naturally, I believed in my work but I have to admit I wasn't sure why I was so obsessed with it, other than that it was mine. Is this what all writers feel after they die and have the time to be objective?

I felt Danni's eyes come alive. I could see that she wanted to say something but stopped herself.

"Also, you know, the guy dies of a heart attack in midsentence. Very cool selling point. Like that kid Jonathan Larson dying on opening night before *Rent* has its world premiere."

"He was working on a rewrite of an awful screenplay," I interjected.

"Okay, not as cool as that but it is something to talk about. Would it be better if he'd been murdered? Yes, but you take what you get."

I nodded. We were done here. I had gotten from Harris what I needed—his enthusiasm, though I wasn't sure if it was sincere or *partially* sincere or he just wanted to get paid. I also realized it didn't matter because I needed his help and he was going to give it. "Which novel did you like best?" I asked casually.

Harris look startled. "Does it matter?"

"Just curious."

Harris was stupefied. Danni looked away.

I realized then that he hadn't read either one.

"*The Dead Mexican*," Danni said.

Doug and I both looked at her.

"Though *The Last Vision* is amazing," she continued.

I smiled. He hadn't read the books; she did. He didn't review the novels; she had.

Harris said when the check came, "You got this," trying to make it sound like a question.

I picked up the check. "I certainly do."

He was out the door in seconds, but Danni lingered and handed me her card without saying anything.

I watched her push her way through the round tables reaching the front door and the hazy sunlight until she wasn't there anymore.

I spent Monday night on the internet looking up everything I could about Warren Fabrizi and Allan Roth. I also read the online versions of *Variety*, *The Hollywood Reporter* and every major publishing blog I could remember. I needed to catch up to the world I had so recently left.

I managed to get a quick meeting with Claudia on Tuesday morning. Her assistant let me in, and I was quickly seated at her desk. She was on her Bluetooth talking to a client when she turned to me and said, "Max, nice to meet you. Glad you're going to publish Tom's books. Can I help in any way?"

"Yes, you can," I told her.

She was startled.

"Can you sell the movie rights to *The Dead Mexican*?"

"I already did," she told me. "And *The Last Vision* has been with Warner Brothers for a year already."

"What about his plays? Any interest in turning them into movies or perhaps you can turn *The Borough Chronicles* into a cable series?"

"There's no interest in Tom's plays," she answered.

I could tell that Claudia found Max physically appealing. Having an eye for men is what broke up her marriage. She liked movie stars, up-and-coming movie stars, and even those on the decline. Claudia was a starfucker.

"Do you have time for cocktails after work?" she asked.

That evening I was sipping a martini with Claudia in a restaurant on Seventh Avenue and Fifty-sixth Street. It was crowded but we managed to find a place at the bar.

I was now watching and examining Claudia in a way Tom Chillo never did. I was doing all that as Max

Foreman. I had never noticed how enticing Claudia's hips were and how she managed to face you when she spoke to you; she turned her body toward yours. As Tom, I noticed how she played with her hair a lot as if she were a teenage girl. I never realized how sensual it was until I was Max. I also took note of how sparkling her eyes were, how she focused them as if she had found an interesting-looking meal, and that meal was Max.

Most important, though she wasn't wearing silver or dusted with glitter, it seemed as if she were. I wasn't sure if it was the restaurant's lighting or the fact that I could see her aura now that I was deceased, but she did sizzle, that's for sure.

"How come I don't know you?" she asked.

I explained that I had never met Tom but loved his work. I told her how I thought he didn't get the recognition he deserved and I wanted to change that.

"Well, I have some bad news for you."

"Like what?"

"The critic Allan Roth is putting together an anthology of American fiction writers of the last fifty years. He has picked twenty-five, and Tom is not one of them. The book is getting a lot of attention and it's not even out yet. Amazon is publishing it and the *Times* is doing a story on it in their magazine section. They plan on really pushing it."

I eyed Claudia as she eyed me. She wasn't as slender as when we first met but she was still alluring. She was so feminine and had a wonderful twinkle of mayhem in her light-brown eyes.

"Allan Roth the critic?" I asked.

"Yes. He has that column in *The New Yorker*. What he doesn't hate he admires. He has no middle ground. Middle ground for him is indifference. He refused to review both of Tom's novels."

I knew this and it was a fact that was hard to swallow.

"There's nothing worse for a writer than complete indifference. Here is my new novel! Presto, who cares? That was basically what Roth wrote back to me when I sent Tom's to him." Claudia told me.

"Write him and tell him he must reconsider," I said.

"Why? He has selected another of my clients. Do you know Kenneth Ungly? Of course you do."

I nodded. I hated Ungly's work. It was clever, insightful, and he was talented. However, it was small-minded. It never reached for anything large or philosophical and when it did, it fell apart. He was on the verge of being a genius but he wasn't one yet. And now Roth was going to give him a leg up on me.

"So, as you can see, I can't cut off my nose to spite my

face," Claudia said.

"Tom adored you," I said sincerely.

Claudia seemed surprised with my sincerity. "How close were you to Tom?"

I shrugged. "As I told you, we never met. But he wrote me over the years. He told me how lucky he was to have you as his agent. I always admired talent and his spoke to me. I have family money and I want to republish his books because I don't want them to disappear. I have Doug Harris writing the foreword, and—"

She cut me off. "Doug doesn't read anything. Danni, his assistant, reads what he should."

"I know." I nodded. "I also met with Sarah, his literary executrix."

"That sad, pathetic case," Claudia said. "She loved him and wasted an entire life doing so." Claudia took a long sip of her martini and put her hand on mine. "What are your plans later? Much later."

"I need to persuade Roth to place Tom in that anthology."

"That's not what I meant," Claudia said.

"It's what I have to do or figure out how to do," I said.

She wrote down an address. I read it and immediately recognized it as hers. She didn't know that I not only knew it, I had been there.

"Come by around eleven."

"Why?" I asked her sharply.

I supposed my being so handsome, and perhaps because she had a weakness for handsome, trim, elegant, and clearly self-possessed men, at first Claudia held her tongue and touched her hair, rolling the ends of it between her fingers. Yet she didn't suffer insults or fools. "'Why?' you ask?"

I aimed my newly cool, merciless eyes on hers but said nothing.

"Perhaps I can help you figure away to get to Roth and at least have a conversation with him."

"When does his anthology go to print?"

"Soon," Claudia answered.

I lifted my chin. I looked at Claudia as if for the first time. I was fighting feelings of profound disappointment. She didn't realize that she had broken what was left of Tom Chillo's heart. Max spoke up in Tom's defense. "I'll be there."

Claudia nodded, picked up the tab, and disappeared out onto the street that wasn't quite dark yet. Just then I saw Warren Fabrizi walking by. I was taken aback but quickly rushed out of the restaurant and followed him into the night.

He walked down Seventh Avenue, and I had to watch

him closely so I wouldn't lose him in the crowd. I focused on his compact frame, his long and thick black hair, and his stride, which always seemed to me oddly erratic. He walked like an engine piston, with his slender shoulders gyrating to one side and then the other and his head bobbing back and forth.

He stopped at a corner waiting for the light and I caught up to him. I gave him a sideways glance and I noticed that he had noticed me, yet he said nothing as he waited for the light. It *was* New York so he might have thought I was someone else but there was something in his look that made me shudder. I wondered if there was any possible chance that he could know I was Tom Chillo, his sworn enemy in death as in life.

I knew it couldn't be possible but I felt a connection that was otherworldly; then again, I was dead and pretending to be someone else.

I caught a glimpse of a theater where I once had a play put on. It had a good run with good reviews and nice-sized audiences. It was a joyous time, an adventure for a young, excitable, and enthusiastic playwright.

The light changed and Fabrizi walked on. I stayed on the corner. I let him go, for now, and I looked back at the theater to enjoy, for one more moment, a happy memory.

CHAPTER 11

I took a cab down to the West Village and met Sarah at Sammy's Noodle Shop & Grill on Sixth Avenue and Eleventh Street, right across the street from French Roast. I was late but she was already halfway through her first glass of wine.

I told her about my meeting with Claudia, which made her a little jealous, and then I told her what Claudia had shared with me about Allan Roth. I wanted to unburden myself of my masquerade. I wanted to also share what I was learning. It was easier to go through life handsome than talented. To be both handsome *and* talented was a gift from the gods.

Sammy's was the place Sarah and I liked to go for Chinese food. Our favorite was the sesame chicken, so I ordered it and was surprised she didn't say anything. I talked about my day with Doug Harris, too. She listened closely and then remarked that Allan Roth was going to be impossible.

"Does he even know Tom's work?" she said.

I sat back and sighed. "We have to get him to know it and like it enough to include it in the anthology."

Our dinner together was not easy. I was uncomfortable and restless. I had a sense of what eternity was going to be like, realizing the possibility that I'd never make it to the hill where the Eternals dwelled. Being with Sarah also made me remember how much time I'd spent with her in my life while itching to be somewhere else, where my life as a writer meant something. I imagined myself walking a red carpet, being with other successful people in the arts, anything but being alone with one person. I knew that just wasn't for me and the older I grew the more obvious it became.

"Why was Tom so obsessed with fame?" Sarah asked, as if she were reading my mind.

"Immortality. He was obsessed with immortality."

"Is there a difference, really?"

"Yes. I can name you writers who were famous in their lifetimes and never achieved *immortality*. I can name you writers who are now immortal but never achieved a bit of fame in their lifetimes. Van Gogh–type writers, I call them. Of course, the majority have some kind of fame and notoriety in their lifetimes but never achieve the greatness that happens to so few," I answered, having learned much of this since going to the Writers Afterlife.

She took a moment then said, "That's something Tom would say."

"It's probably how he thought."

"Sad but true. It is exactly how he thought. I was never enough for him. Actually, no woman was ever enough for him. No person, not even his family was enough for him."

I absorbed what she said and nodded.

"Let me ask you this. If he did, let's say, become a Mark Twain, would he have been satisfied?"

"Does a Tolstoy know he's a Tolstoy?" I asked.

Sarah nodded. "Probably somewhere in time he does."

"What do you think, Sarah? Would Tom have been satisfied knowing that being Tom Chillo meant something?"

She took a moment. She was a smart woman who tried not to think too much about things that hurt. I always thought about things that hurt. It was my job to do that. It was the kind of writer I was. I wrote about loneliness, loss, and betrayal.

"He wrote about loneliness, loss, and betrayal," I said. "Tom would have been content but like the poet Delmore

Schwartz who had this interesting notion about fame. To paraphrase, what was good about being famous was that you didn't have to tell other people that you were. You didn't have to look for validation. It came to you from others."

Sarah studied me intently. "He never paid attention to my loneliness."

"Are you sure about that?"

Sarah stopped talking and continued eating. I watched how she used her chopsticks, remembering how she used to use them when I was alive, and felt a pang of sadness for her and for myself. I'd never cheated on her but I broke her heart in a hundred ways.

After dinner I once again found myself standing in front of Sarah's small apartment on a pretty street in the West Village in the dark as I had for so many nights.

"He never liked sleeping over," she told me.

"Some people like their own bed."

"He took Ambien, for Christ's sake, and he still didn't stay over much. Tom wasn't normal!"

"Writers aren't," I told her.

I saw it was important for her to confide in me. I understood why she felt close to Max Foreman: he was close to the now-dead Tom Chillo whom she loved more than anything else. What I didn't understand was how she could share the intimate agony with a stranger who hadn't shown her any compassion or sympathy other than a few words of encouragement.

"I'm only here one more day. Did you think about handing Claudia the position of executrix? That way, perhaps, she can find some literary person at the Authors Guild to represent Tom's work?"

Sarah said, "I want to remain executrix."

"But you don't have plans to do anything with his work," I said quickly.

"I'll come up with something. There's time," she said, then turned her back on me and entered her building.

I wanted to tell her that there wasn't any time and I knew that better than anyone else, but before I could say another word, the door had closed.

———

When I got to her building and told the doorman my name, he grinned and sent me right up.

Claudia was sitting on her sofa in the dim light of her table lamp surrounded by scripts she had been reading and the program to an Off-Broadway musical. I had no desire to seduce or to even be seduced, but I could see she sure had the desire to seduce Max Foreman.

"Writers. Such an odd group. I wonder if it's in their DNA or their upbringing or in their souls. I have spent my life representing them and I'm still not sure what they're made of. Some are cold-blooded but they write the most beautiful poetry. Some are drunks and/or drug addicts but write the most elegant prose. Others are brilliant screenwriters but lack the fire and guts to direct. Others hide behind everything they write."

"And Tom?"

Claudia slugged down her drink. I realized she was sitting down because she was drunk. "What about him?"

"What kind of writer was he?"

"He wasn't as talented as he thought he was."

Cruel, I thought. "Why do you say that?"

"I don't know. I thought he had moments of brilliance. There are passages in *The Dead Mexican* that are just breathtaking. The beginning, the opening scene of *The Last Vision* has never left me since the day I first read it. And yet I thought there was so much more he could do."

I sat near her. I didn't want to get too close but I needed to hear more. "How do you mean?"

"He wrote so much, but it never seemed to stick. I mean, he published so many plays and his residuals were never substantial."

"He made a living his entire adult life as a writer. And he made money for you with his rewrite work."

"He made lots of money for the both of us," she said.

"So, why don't you think he was a great writer?" I asked.

Claudia ignored my question as if she hadn't heard it, reached up, and kissed me. It was an awkward kiss mainly because she was drunk but not entirely for that reason.

I felt so odd kissing her.

"Enough about Tom. I want to talk about you."

I shook my head. "I want to talk about Allan Roth."

A few moments later we were standing on her very narrow balcony overlooking Fourteenth Street and Union Square. The view was at an odd angle but the park was there. The noise swept up from the streets below and I could hear bits of conversations, teenagers shouting, loud voices rising up and out of the concrete canyon below. I could see the pedestrians on the sidewalk in the crazy mix of streetlights and storefront lights and the horizontal glow from car headlights. It was a lonely city and nobody escaped the pull of that emptiness. Not even the dead.

She had her arm around my waist. "Twelve stories up and I feel I'm a million miles away," she said.

"I need to meet Allan Roth."

"Were you in love with Tom or something?" she asked.

I smiled. "Sort of."

"I didn't think you were gay."

"I'm not. I love the man's work," I told her. I was pushing the limits. I knew that. But truth was the best lie and I had to keep up the façade. I needed to get to Roth.

"Even if I did set up a meeting, he'd eat you alive."

"Do you really think that?" I said, confidently.

Claudia looked at me. I could see the glare of lights in her eyes, I could see a hunger in her look I'd never seen before when I was Tom Chillo. Life had distracted me; death seemed to focus all that I had missed. Before, I'd scanned life though a telescope; now, I was looking at it through a microscope. It was frightening but I didn't have time to react to fear.

"I want to suck you off, Max."

I reacted to her words but not how she wanted to. I backed away from her. Before I could do anything else, I felt her hands touching my shoulders, my arms, and then my crotch.

Claudia pulled my penis out from inside my pants. She played with it a bit, rubbing it up and down and smiling at me. "I feel like tasting you, I really do," she said.

But it wasn't *my* penis she was handling quite expertly, it Max Foreman's. I looked down at it. Of course, I had given Max a big cock. I gave Max everything I didn't have in real life: good looks, a calm exterior, and a big dick.

"Wow, nice," Claudia said. I didn't really know how to take the compliment. Max Foreman was a creation of my imagination. Everything about him existed because I made him that way. So now, as he was getting a blow job from my promiscuous agent, I was feeling, well, put off. "God, you're nice and *big*," Claudia whispered and then began to suck Max off.

I knew she never even considered sucking *my* penis. And if she did, would this highly critical, world-weary, sophisticated, and very hip literary agent ever compliment my penis while giving me a blow job? I doubted it.

Thank God I had talent, I said to myself. I had something Max Foreman didn't have: a body of literary work under my name. Well, it wasn't actually an impressive body of work since it consisted mainly of two novels, some plays, and a few feature film credits, but I did have talent.

Max's reason for existing had only to do with making Tom Chillo famous and if he enjoyed having a large penis, so be it. I was glad I gave him one and fought against comparing his dick with mine as much as I could, despite the circumstances: my creation getting head from someone I'd known a very long time and had never slept with.

It was then that I allowed myself to feel Claudia's mouth sucking away. At first I sensed it was all about desire but I quickly realized that I was wrong; it was actually all about loneliness. Eventually, she slowed down but the intensity didn't. In a matter of minutes, I came, or more succinctly, Max came, and Claudia got up from her knees and walked back into the apartment, alone.

—⁓—

I looked out over what I could see of the city, facing downtown. I thought of all the lives that stumbled through the night—most, if not all, in denial of death. I knew I'd written because I loved life, not because I feared death.

"You'll have one shot with him. Just one," Claudia said, stepping back onto the balcony, puffing on a cigarette. "He'll be at a party for PEN International at the Pierre tomorrow night. You're in luck because after that he flies off to Paris."

She handed me an invitation. "You can come along with me as my guest."

I nodded slowly.

"Now go," she said.

When I reached the street it occurred to me that I would have to leave life by midnight on Wednesday night. That didn't leave much time other than perhaps a few minutes to speak to Allan Roth.

I also realized that my plan of breaking my trip into two parts might actually work for me. I could always return to life whenever I thought best: a month from now, a year, or ten years. It was up to me to make that decision. It would naturally depend on how much progress I made now.

I turned south on Broadway and walked toward Tribeca when I received a text. It was from Danni. She wanted to have breakfast with me tomorrow morning at seven. Because I didn't need sleep I had no problem with that, so I suggested my hotel.

She texted me back immediately with a smiling face.

I spent most of the night standing at the corner of White Street at the hotel's entrance in front of the big clock designed to look like an antique. I leaned against the old fashioned lampposts, then walked up White Street, then to Canal Street, then west to Varick Street, and down to Worth and Church Streets, allowing the city and its dead souls wash over me. It was an ugly quiet, the kind that makes no sense because the quiet comes from nowhere in particular.

It was odd being a ghost. Though others saw me and spoke to me, they had no idea that I was not real. I looked like flesh and blood; if a doctor examined me, he or she would find a heart and a liver and all the necessary organs human beings need, but they wouldn't be real and no X-ray machine could show the doctor that. Of course, the writer's imagination made everything, even a sexual orgasm, possible.

I stayed up all night thinking what I could say to Roth and guessing what Danni had to tell me. I was running out of time.

CHAPTER 12

Danni was right on time and perky. I noticed she dressed up for our meeting, allowing herself to look more feminine than she did around Harris. Though there wasn't much she could do with her very short blond hair, I felt like we were more on a date than a business meeting even thought the sun hadn't been up very long.

I found us a table near the window and away from the din of voices. We had some quick chitchat and then she told me that she, not Doug, was going to write the foreword.

I didn't react but I thought it was a good thing because she seemed pleased. "I can have it for you whenever you need it."

"But I'm paying Doug and I need his name on it."

"His name will be on it and he will take care of me, so not to worry." She smiled and drank her fresh orange juice.

"And why are you doing this?"

"It's my job. And I want to help."

"I appreciate it," I told her.

"You seem sincere in your conviction about Tom Chillo's work. I believe it's warranted."

I sipped my coffee and felt the wheels of my own brain turning. "I'm hoping to meet Allan Roth tonight. He's putting together an anthology of the best fiction writers of the last twenty-five years, and Tom is *not* included."

Danni listened closely, smiling at me with her bright eyes.

"I'll have only seconds to grab his attention so that he pays attention to me. How do I persuade him to include Tom? I'd love your opinion on this."

Danni grew quiet. She was a very deliberate woman. I could see her thought processes, the way she took her time, mulled it over, examining every detail. Now I knew why Doug Harris kept her as his assistant. What Danni possessed was indispensable to someone as volatile and impulsive as he was.

Then I noticed that Danni was now looking at me differently. I realized she had developed a crush on Max

Foreman. She struggled, thought some more, started to say something, and then tensed up.

"Take some time, Danni," I told her. "We have some. Not a lot but some."

Danni collected her thoughts by keeping her lips close together and her eyes fixated on nothing in particular and then she spoke up. "Allan Roth prefers writers like Proust and Joyce and Melville and Beckett. He likes writers who write about writing. It's easier to be a critic and expound on the art when you discuss Thomas Pynchon and David Foster Wallace. You sound smarter than your readers and Roth lives for that.

"You can't write pages and pages on Stephen King or even a great storyteller like Dickens without talking plot and character and story structure. Allan Roth equates novels with plots to television writing, which is absurd, because one is written by committee and the other by an individual who has struggled with a theme and works to see how plot can emphasize that premise. There is a lot of craft to that, but he doesn't find it intriguing.

"So, as you know, Tom wrote good plots but he had metaphors and such exceptional dialogue that his work transcends potboilers. You have to make Roth see the value in that, and I don't know how you do it. He's a prickly man. The word is he's not gay or straight but

asexual if that is possible. So give me until the afternoon if that's okay, Max?"

I nodded. "Of course."

"Do you have a room here?" She asked.

"Yes."

"I've never seen the rooms here. Are they nice?" she
asked almost politely.

———

The window in my room faced the industrial landscape
of the once-thriving factory buildings and truck-loading stops
of the previous century. Those buildings and loading stops
were now artifacts turned into co-ops and high-tech offices.

I closed the door, looked at Danni, and shrugged.
"When do you have to get back to your office?" I asked.

"I have time," Danni answered. She walked over to
me and touched my face, looked up into my eyes, then
turned. She leaned over the bed and then pulled down
her skirt, then her panties, offering me, Max, her petite
round bottom. "Do you have a condom? Please say yes."

"I'm not sure about this," I told her.

"I am. I like you, Max," Danni said her face still directed
away from me.

A condom materialized in my hand. I just willed it to
be there. Then I pulled Max's penis out of his pants and
put on the condom and quickly entered her. Danni had

sex like she worked and lived. It was intense, deliberate, and there was a time limit. I watched as she closed her eyes and gripped the bedspread. I put my hands firmly on her hips and rocked back and forth, listening to her moan ever so slightly. She was using me to get off. She dropped her face onto the bed, keeping her bottom in the air even after I pulled out of her.

She lay silent for a few moments, then quickly stood, pulled up her panties, and adjusted her skirt. She looked at me and again touched my face. "You're so beautiful."

She then gathered her things and walked to the door. "I will e-mail you a catchy phrase or an opening line to hook Roth before your dinner at the Pierre," she told me, then left.

I closed the door and sat down on the bed. I was having more sex as a ghost than when I actually existed.

Later that afternoon Danni came through for me. She e-mailed me as she said she would.

I sat with Claudia who did what all agents do well at social events. She spoke to everyone at the table, shemoved around the event making sure she dropped names, mentioned her current clients' achievements, and had her antenna up, listening to all that could help her find her clients work.

She looked terrific in a business skirt but her hair, once lovely and wavy, no longer fell over her shoulders but instead was pulled back. It made her look severe and less vivacious.

I spent the cocktail hour searching for Allan Roth and eventually, when I did find him, I realized I couldn't actually get close enough to speak with him. He was surrounded by so many others vying for his attention.

While biding time, I pretended I was interested in what was served for dinner. I smiled at those who smiled at me and did my best to continue small talk with Claudia but all I really wanted was to be alone with Allan Roth. I eyed him like a hawk perched on a hilltop measuring its prey's every move.

Eventually, I got my wish. I followed him into the men's room. It was nearly empty other than the attendant in a bad tuxedo who handed out cologne and towels.

I pretended to walk up to the urinal. We were standing in the far corner of the large restroom. Roth was in his late fifties, more than just balding; the only hair he had left on his head was stringy and brown and stuck to the back of his collar. Though his blue eyes were small, they were very cold and caught me looking directly at him from across the brightly lit men's room.

He looked like the kind of man the police arrest for exposing themselves to schoolgirls. He had all the proper and unattractive clichéd looks of an academic who was more comfortable in a proper library setting but secretly longed to find a peephole in the janitor's office to give him a pervert's view of the ladies' room.

"Mr. Roth," I said.

He turned to me and I could see that the impressive, handsome presence of Max Foreman had gotten his attention.

"You were Tom Chillo's favorite critic," I said.

"I'm nearly everyone's favorite critic," he replied.

"He said you were the only critic who truly understood Dante's *Inferno*."

"Really?"

"He said you believed Dante saw himself as Satan and was actually punishing God for never making him famous in his lifetime."

"Who are you?" he asked. He washed his hands at the sink and took a towel.

"Max Foreman. I'm publishing Chillo's two novels and I'd love for you to include an excerpt from one of them in your new anthology."

"I already chose my authors," Roth said and walked out without leaving a tip.

I followed him out and confronted him before he reached the noisy banquet area. "Drop Ungly and include Chillo."

Roth now turned on me. "Who the *hell* are you?"

"I'm Max Foreman. A great fan of Chillo's."

Roth now eyed me with great concern. He turned and walked away. I grabbed his shoulder. He stopped and spun around toward me. I could see the look of recognition in his eyes. "You're not Max Foreman, whoever that is."

"What?" I said, taken aback.

"Fraud."

I was unable to react.

"I know exactly who you are."

He narrowed his eyes to make sure I got his point. "You're the author. You are Tom Chillo."

"Tom Chillo is dead."

He shook his head. "You're *Tom Chillo*. You're from the Writers Afterlife."

With that he was gone.

I left the Pierre after my confrontation with Allan Roth and walked up Fifth Avenue along Central Park. I needed the silence and privacy of that neighborhood where the exclusively rich lived in their isolation.

How did Allan Roth even know there was a Writers Afterlife? How did Allan Roth guess who I was?

Somewhere in my walk between one lamppost and another, at the stroke of midnight I walked into a shadow and I disappeared back to the Writers Afterlife.

CHAPTER 13

Her name was Lucy and she was sitting across from me. We were sitting at a wooden table on a hill in the bright and lovely sunlight. Lucy had taken Joe's place as my guide.

"How did Allan Roth know that was me?" I asked.

Lucy explained. "He *is* a major critic. He has been approached before by other dead writers."

Lucy had a pleasant, round face with bright soft brown eyes and Slavic features. She spoke slowly but intelligently and listened to everything I had to say.

When we met, she explained to me that she'd been a ballerina in Russia in the 1910s and had been one of the royal palace's favorites, but then the Revolution happened. She was only a passerby but soldiers fired at the crowd and a bullet hit her directly in the forehead. She died on the street in the freshly fallen snow.

She had been ready to move to Paris where she knew she would be internationally famous, as she was the best-known ballet dancer in Moscow at the time, having also danced in Florence and Vienna. Her death stopped her from being famous. I wondered how she thought that she would someday be famous and she had an answer.

"One day they will make a movie about me in Russia," she smiled. "The world will then know about me."

I changed the subject back to Roth. "And one of these writers told him all about the Writers Afterlife and how it all *happens* here?"

Lucy nodded. "Yes. And that writer was severely punished. He was denied his remaining time in life."

She was only twenty-one when she died and she was twenty-one when she was speaking to me. I could sense that she knew I needed some answers and some reassurance. I also sensed that her duty was to quiet me down.

I was obviously annoyed. I got up and paced back and forth. "I didn't know someone could *tell*. Why didn't you people explain that to me?"

"No need knowing something you didn't need to know."

I was fuming. I now had to come up with a new plan.

Lucy tried to calm me down with the truth. "Tom, when an artist goes back they can do more than just tell someone. You met the playwright Jack. He actually killed that director friend of his," Lucy told me.

"He did? I mean, he was telling me the truth?"

"He certainly was," Lucy explained.

"I didn't believe him when he told me."

"Believe him. Some artists go back into their lives and wreck havoc on the living. They did it in life and they do it in death." Lucy's voice remained steady. "This writer who told it all to Roth became desperate. He saw his time dwindling. He realized that there was a good chance he would never become famous. So, he was scared and told the drunken Roth the truth. You can imagine that, can't you?"

I stopped pacing. "Yes, I can, but what does that mean to me now? The fact that Roth knows that Max Foreman is actually Tom Chillo kills my plan."

"Maybe or maybe not."

"What does that mean?"

Lucy elaborated. "Perhaps you can use that to your advantage. It's happened before."

"It has?"

"Don't you know the story of Edgar Allan Poe?"

"The poet who wrote 'The Raven' and 'The Tell-Tale Heart.' Yes, I know of him and his work. He had this happen to him?"

"He was younger than you when you died. He was only forty."

"No shit? And he's famous. Really famous. I mean, the French love him! He's supposed to be thought of as the first to create the detective story in the English language. He's so famous that he is actually a character in other people's stories. I mean, he embodies the notion of haunted and the insane. He is also the most famous pedophile ever. He married his thirteen-year-old cousin, for God's sake. So, what about Poe?"

—⁓—

Lucy and I were now in a pub. It was raining outside. I didn't see anyone else in the pub, not even a bartender, when Lucy nudged me. She gestured to a slender man with thick black hair seemingly stuck to his square forehead and a thick black mustache across his upper lip sitting alone at a corner table. His black eyes were staring ahead into the shadows. He didn't even notice us.

Everything smelled of damp wood. The fireplace to the left of us was losing heat and light. Shadows danced on the walls.

"Is that Poe?" I asked.

"No, it's not," Lucy said.

"I was sure it's him. He's one of the few writers that people can actually recognize."

Lucy's eyes lit up. "Poe died on a rainy night and his body was found along a railroad track. Nobody knows what or who killed him. Some say he had cerebral inflammation brought on by extreme alcoholism. Others believe he was murdered. But it doesn't matter," Lucy explained. "The only thing that matters is that when he died he was not as famous as he is today."

"Really?"

Lucy turned to me and said in earnest. "Did you ever hear of Rufus Griswold?"

"Who was he?"

"He is the man who *made* Poe famous."

Lucy gestured to the man at the table.

"That's Griswold?" I asked.

Lucy nodded. Griswold looked exactly like Poe in the dim light. But when I looked closer I could see that his hair wasn't as dark as I first thought.

Griswold moved his right hand. He used it to lift a small cup to his lips, drink whatever it was he had in it, then place the cup back on the table. A black top hat sat on the chair next to him and behind him was a window.

Through it I could see the wind move the larger branches on the trees waving back and forth.

"Griswold died pretty much like Poe. He died drunk along railroad tracks outside Baltimore in the rain only a few years after Poe died," Lucy explained.

"How did he make Poe famous?"

Lucy told me. "The day after Poe died an article appeared in the *New-York Tribune*. It basically said that Poe had died the night before and though many will be surprised, only few will grieve. It was signed 'Ludwig.'"

"Who was Ludwig?"

"Ludwig was Griswold," Lucy answered.

I turned back to Griswold. Lucy continued. "Griswold and Poe had some kind of feud. No one knows what it was about. Most say it was just one writer being jealous of another. Funny thing, Griswold was publishing more than Poe was. Poe was living in dire poverty despite publishing 'The Pit and the Pendulum' and 'Annabel Lee.'"

"That story and that poem are both classics today. Every high school student has read them. They made movies out of them. And we have Rufus Griswold to thank for that?"

Lucy nodded. "Yes."

I figured it out. "Poe left the Writers Afterlife to confront Griswold in life."

"Exactly!" Lucy said. "Poe waited in the Valley for about a year and his name took a dip into obscurity. Then he took his one-week opportunity to go back to life. And do know what his motivation was?"

I shook my head.

"After Poe's death Griswold managed to become executor of Poe's work."

"No way!"

Lucy smiled. "Yes. Through his own tireless machinations and the indifference from Poe's estate, Griswold secured the rights to all of Poe's work. And then in 1850, only one year after Poe's death, Griswold published a volume of Poe's collected works and within it he published a biographical essay entitled 'Memoir of the Author.' In it he depicted Poe as a depraved, drunk madman. He wanted to destroy what existed of Poe's literary reputation." Lucy said. "And in the memoir he included letters written by Poe as evidence."

I looked at Griswold, dressed as Poe would dress in a dark jacket, black vest, and white shirt. "Griswold didn't have to exaggerate that much. Poe was a madman, wasn't he?" I asked.

Lucy shook her head. "The letters were a forgery. All of Griswold's claims were lies or only half-truths."

"Really?"

"Yes." Lucy could see my reaction.

I made a face. Life felt so ironic to me and so absurd. This entire story seemed so bizarre.

"'Memoir of the Author' became immensely popular. And, as it was the only full biography of Poe available to readers, it made Poe instantly famous in death and created such an intensely drawn image of a poetic, drug-fueled, sexual madman, Poe the deceased suddenly became Poe the icon. Though Poe's friends argued that what Griswold wrote was a lie, it didn't matter. The letters only added fuel to the public's love of the macabre. Poe's sincere recurring themes of death were now connected to the living, breathing image of the haunted soul."

I glanced at Griswold. He still hadn't acknowledged us. "And all this means *what* concerning my situation?" I asked.

Lucy leaned in close to me so I could see her pale skin and gentle features. "It was Poe who appeared to Griswold and gave him the idea of writing the 'Memoir.'"

"It was Poe's idea to write those crazy lies about himself?"

Lucy continued. "One night, Poe showed up looking like the walking dead. He was dressed all in black with a black cap to highlight the gloom and otherworldliness. Can you imagine Griswold's reaction? There he is sitting at the fireplace and Poe walks through his door. It was 'The Tell-Tale Heart' all over again."

Just then, Griswold got up, turned, and walked out the back door. He left it open. I got up and followed him with Lucy right behind me. We both stood at the open door looking out at a small, dark figure of a man stepping down into a gully heading toward railroad tracks. Lightning flashed and thunder barreled through the rainy night.

"So Poe appeared as an apparition, a ghost from the grave, and made Griswold write those lies about him, and in doing that he created the famous image of the haunted, demented, drug-fueled, sex-addicted, infamous Edgar Allan Poe who fell in love with dead young girls," I stated.

Lucy nodded. "Yes, Tom. That's exactly it."

"And all those stories and poems about the grotesque were connected to a haunted man and that image gave those lines more potency and assured Poe a place in the Writers Afterlife," I concluded.

We walked back to our table, shutting the door before we did.

"Poe knew how to market himself. None of it was true. Well, he was wild and crazy and he did have some unnatural stirrings including those of a sexual nature for a beautiful young female corpse as you said, but what the hell, it made him very famous," Lucy said.

"And what happened to Griswold?" I asked.

"He tried to tell people his story. He hung out in pubs like this the rest of his short life telling anyone who'd listen to him that Poe's ghost appeared to him. But no one believed him. He soon realized the irony of his plight. His need to exact revenge on Poe backfired and made Poe so famous that no one cared about Griswold."

I nodded and grinned. "Wow, I'm learning more about the famous now that I'm dead then when I was alive."

———

Moments later Lucy and I were in the Valley where the sun was right above us and the sky was clear.

"Is Griswold here?" I asked.

"No, Griswold isn't and never was on the verge of being anything but Poe's biggest enemy, and then ironically the catalyst that made Poe a famous writer."

"I want to see Poe."

Lucy contemplated a moment. "You aren't allowed to go where the Eternals are. You know that," she said.

"Exceptions seem to be the norm here. From what I just learned and how I need to appear before Allan Roth next time, I'd like to talk to Poe a minute," I said.

It was only seconds later when I was alone watching Edgar Allan Poe standing in front of a large house set back from a line of trees. A big, black raven was perched on Poe's right arm as he spoke to it in poetic meter. I had never seen eyes so large and black, not only on the Raven but on Poe! He didn't just look haunted—he *was* haunted.

I walked up to him and he turned to me when I reached him. "I had to meet you."

Poe nodded silently.

"So you appeared to Griswold, you told him you were a ghost from the Writers Afterlife, and then you made him write every word of your 'Memoir'?"

Poe let the raven fly away and then he turned to me. "I wrote every word of that 'Memoir.' That's why it was so popular. It was in my voice. Can you honestly believe Griswold had an inkling of talent to mimic me?" Poe asked with a high, strained voice.

It was odd seeing him in the bright sunshine. He was dressed all in black but he looked oddly content. "Of course not," I answered.

Poe smiled. "That is why it was such a popular book. I wrote every word. I created every outrageous false concoction about myself from inhaling opiates to seeing Satan in a loincloth. I had such fun that night, making up that 'Memoir.'"

"Where was Griswold when you were doing that?"

"He was kneeling in the corner, praying. He swallowed an entire bottle of a bad port to get through that night. When the sun came up and I was done writing, I

told him to publish it. I threatened that if he didn't publish it, I'd return with Lucifer himself and haunt
Griswold's days and nights for however long he lived."

The door opened and a very pretty, very young lady
stepped out of the house. "Annabel," Poe called out. He
smiled to himself and waved her over. He turned back to
me. "The biography made me famous and got me out of
the Valley to dwell here where I belong, with the Eternals."

I nodded and quickly left him alone with his Annabel.

CHAPTER 14

After my return to the Valley, the days and nights, the thing we call time, became more real for me than anything else. I did all I could to be patient. I worked on my plan to return to life for three and half more days and take my one last shot at immortality.

The problem I faced was determining how long I should wait before I headed back. I took care of the things I had to while I was there: Doug Harris got his money; he delivered his wonderful foreword, no doubt written by his astute assistant, Danni; and with Sarah's help, I actually republished a two-book release of my own novels, *The Dead Mexican* and *The Last Vision*.

I left an e-mail for Sarah that I returned to Canada and though she wrote me several times, I never wrote back. I never bothered contacting Claudia before I left, and thought long and hard about Allan Roth—if I should pull an Edgar Allan Poe on him and make him my Rufus Griswold. But I realized that unlike Griswold, who hated Poe, Roth didn't hate me. He just didn't think I was worthy of his attention as a critic.

———

"Do you know Warren Fabrizi? He's a novelist and playwright who also wrote some movies?" Lucy asked me. We were sitting in a wonderful café in Paris. I wanted to be in Paris so I made Paris appear and there we were.

"Yes, I know Warren. He's not a friend but an acquaintance."

"Well, he's dating Sarah now."

It was about six months after Max Foreman had visited life and I wasn't paying much attention to what was going on back there because I was slowly adjusting to living in the Valley of Those on the Verge. What gradually happened was that you slowly became more and more accepting of your fate. You became sedate. You knew how hard it was to change anything so you did all you could to forget.

"Warren Fabrizi is sleeping with Sarah and working diligently to make sure that she hands over the authority of executor of your work to him. He is doing this by telling her that he knows how to market your work, is friends with Doug Harris, is in communication with Allan Roth, and just signed with Claudia Wilson."

Hearing all this devastated me. "He's pulling a Rufus Griswold," I said.

A year flew by in life but in the Writers Afterlife nothing flew by in that same way; everything was in a perpetual state of "in the moment," meaning that there was no sense of past and yesterday and no sense of tomorrow and the future. The only thing that existed was a moment, a pure moment in which you existed.

I tried finding Jennifer again, but for a so-called long time she didn't want to see me. Suddenly, one afternoon, there she was and the two of us were sitting in a convertible in Malibu driving north on the Pacific Coast Highway, with the sun slowly setting into the sea.

"Thank you for being here. This is my favorite place in the world, driving with the top down in the sunshine and ocean breeze," she said.

"Glad to be here," I said. "I'd been looking for you."

She smiled. "I know."

The next moment we were sitting on a picnic bench at a roadside café. There was sand at her feet and coffee in large mugs in front of us. There was a menu on the wall written in bold, colorful chalk announcing the specials of the day.

"I'm going back soon," she told me. "I have a plan. I can't talk about it much, but an anthology of Asian women writers is apparently being published. They chose one of my stories."

"That's great. What year are you going back?" I asked.

"2014," she said.

"That's the time I'm going back, too," I said. "What city?"

"New York," she answered. "My friend Sue is still there. I'll go back as one of my long-lost nieces and see if I can get Sue to become literary executrix.

"Yes," I said.

"Of course, they have Amy Tan and Gish Jen and Iris Chang."

"Iris Chang committed suicide," I said.

"I know. I saw her up here. Well, I hadn't realized there were so few Asian female writers who are famous so I have a good chance of getting my novels reviewed again," Jennifer said, clearly trying to remain confident.

"How many novels did you publish, again?" I asked, knowing very well it had been twice as many as I'd published.

She looked dejected. "Don't do that to me. Don't let me get myself down. I can't punish myself for all eternity for driving drunk that night. If I hadn't killed myself, Tom, I would have lived and written so much more, I know it."

"I'm sorry."

"You did it on purpose."

I did. It was awful of me but even though I had feelings for Jennifer, she was a writer. I was competitive even in death with someone who hadn't even been a contemporary of mine.

She knew I was sorry. She reached across the table and took my hand. She smiled. "I forgive you."

"What is your specific plan?" I asked.

"Well, Mark is living in San Francisco now, so I won't run into him. I will go back as myself, but will tell my publisher that I am Jennifer Han's long-lost niece and that I want my aunt's novels to be promoted as originals, the first feminist Asian novels. Amy Tan is all about kissing white men's asses, while my novels are about going it alone despite being a drinker and a promiscuous woman. All those things I was."

"And remember all those already up there who only wrote one novel," I told Jennifer. "Harper Lee, Boris Pasternak, Ralph Ellison, Emily Brontë, Oscar Wilde."

I could see her eyes light up.

Moments or hours later, we were in a bedroom in a penthouse overlooking the harbor in Hong Kong. It was twilight and Jennifer was naked and I was naked lying beside her. It was so odd because it was Tom Chillo, dead now for over a year, who was yearning and lusting for Jennifer Han, dead for fifteen years, in bed in a fading twilight of the Far East, yet it was as real as if we had met at Elaine's on the Upper East Side in the 1980s or at Delmonico's on South William Street in 1910 and we were young lovers sharing our hopes and burning ambitions.

We made love slowly; I had no thoughts about my cock and its comparison to Max Foreman's. What was happening was driven by lust, not competition, or so I believed.

I enjoyed feeling her hands touching me with a hunger I hadn't known from her before. I wanted her to move her hands and her tongue anywhere she wanted. I wanted her to feel me and lick me everywhere, as if the more intimate she was with my body, the less difficult it would be for her to become real again back in life, if only for a week.

I turned her around, pulled back her long, black hair, kissed her neck, then kissed the small of her back and the cheeks of her soft bottom, spreading them, licking her vagina from behind, feeling how moist she was, hearing her groan, feeling her hand on my penis, then I was shoving it hard into her, thrusting just enough so that her toes curled and she moaned. She turned her face toward mine, her black eyes nearly white with concentration as if memorizing my own eyes, my features, hoping to make sense out of the reality that two ghosts were actually making love in a city that actually didn't exist for them in the twilight of a time that actually was not occurring in a universe born from our own imaginations.

Jennifer and I tried our best to make sense of the desire we were feeling for each other despite our knowing that we were both in this penthouse bedroom as figments of our own individual imaginations, connected by our deeply instilled loneliness forced upon us by destiny, the unnerving knowledge that we were in a perpetual limbo or perhaps a purgatory, which we were unable to escape from and would be our home for all time—unless, of course, we became famous.

I turned her back around and kissed her passionately, feeling her tongue on mine, feeling both her hands pulling at my own bottom, forcing me to push as deeply into her as I could until neither one of us could wait anymore and we both climaxed.

Sometime later we lay naked on the bed looking down at the lighted ships floating in the dark harbor's water and we watched Hong Kong's unsettling skyline while holding hands, our legs intertwined. I felt her hip and said aloud that it was cruel what death did to us.

"How do I stop wanting you?" I asked her.

"I asked myself the same thing. How do I stop wanting you, Tom?"

"I just made love to a ghost. I desire someone who doesn't exist anymore, other than in her paragraphs and dialogue and in her short stories, poems, and novels. They are playing a joke on us," I said.

Jennifer then turned to me. It was dark now, but I could see her nose and her lips and her dark eyes, all facing me. "If you go back that same week that I am there, please meet me on the corner of Spring Street and Mott at ten at night on February ninth," she said. "I used to know a café there. If it's not there anymore, just meet me on the corner."

"You wouldn't recognize me. I'll be Max Foreman."

"I'll recognize you anywhere you go, no matter who you look like, no matter who you are pretending to be. Trust me. And if not, I'll trust that you will find me."

"Should we really do this?" I asked.

"I want to love you as a living human being in life, not here in this twilight of our souls," she replied. "Even if only for a few hours, I want to be with you in true flesh and blood."

———

We said good-bye to each other in the most romantic setting we both could imagine. It was at a train station in London. It might have been Waterloo Station, as I had been there once. It was eight o'clock on an autumn evening.

My train arrived first, so I was waiting to board while holding her hand.

"You may become famous and enter the place of the Eternals. If that happens to you and not to me, you'll have to leave me behind," she whispered.

"Or the same can happen to you," I told her.

"I don't think the Eternals can visit those in the Valley," she said.

"I know. And I also figure they don't want to. They are so completely happy up there they don't need anything or anyone else," I said.

She agreed. "They receive all their love from their accomplishments. It's like an eternal fountain of warmth."

My train was about to pull out. I hugged Jennifer and she hugged me back. I buried my face in her neck, relishing the feel of her long hair washing over me. Her lips found my mouth and she kissed me. She then pulled away.

I was on the last stair of the train as it pulled out of the station watching Jennifer standing alone under the lamppost on the platform, watching me, not moving, not even waving. She stood there for a long time and I didn't move either. My eyes remained glued to her as she slowly became a figure in the shadows, and eventually nothing more than a ghost I believed I loved and desired, and then moments after that, she was back to what she was, nothing at all.

CHAPTER 15

I returned to New York City in the winter of 2014 on a Wednesday morning at dawn. It was a cold day. The sun shot rays of light through dark gray clouds, and there was a thin layer of ice and frozen snow on the sidewalk.

Naturally, I was Max Foreman again. This time I appeared back in New York City with a couple of copies of the two-book set of Tom Chillo's novels.

My first meeting of the day was with Claudia. She looked pleased to see me but curious that I hadn't been in touch with her in the past year and a half.

"Where have you been?" she asked.

"Up north, working on this," I said handing her the well-designed books.

"I see. You don't get e-mails in Canada?" she said sarcastically.

"I had nothing important to write you back about," I answered in my purely Canadian monotone accent.

She looked the set over. "I like the covers."

"I had someone up in Toronto design them," I told her. The covers were truly well conceived. I had designed them; I knew the novels better than anyone. On the cover of *The Last Vision* an old man's pair of eyes peers through the dark, with a crescent moon hanging over a city skyline and a man sitting at a desk writing, with his free hand fingering a bottle of whiskey. What made the cover work so well was that the man's face was transposed on his own face as a younger man.

The Dead Mexican cover showed a young Mexican woman standing at the United States–Mexico border facing a fierce-looking U.S. Border Patrol guard with sunglasses, holding up her visa. She is clearly vulnerable and sad as she tries to enter the country. What I think made the cover effective was the coffin behind the border checkpoint that she has clearly come to collect.

"Any progress with any of Tom's work?" I asked.

"Some," she told me. "Warren Fabrizi, a wonderful screenwriter and award-winning playwright, is now Tom's literary executor."

"How did that happen?" I asked, displaying just a little too much annoyance.

"Warren and Sarah are now a couple. She felt he knew his way around the literary world better than she did. So she named him executor."

"Weren't Tom and Warren competitors? Didn't they compete for the same prizes, productions, and awards?"

Claudia listened but didn't answer, meaning the answer was yes.

"So that's the progress?" I asked sharply.

"Warren is pitching *The Dead Mexican* as a movie to Warner Brothers and he's going to do the screenplay adaptation. He is also pitching *The Last Vision* as a cable TV series. That should give Tom's work some notoriety," Claudia said.

"Did you ever hear of Rufus Griswold?" I asked.

"No. Is he a producer?" she asked.

I changed the conversation. "What about Allan Roth? What's going on with his anthology?" Actually, I already knew a lot of what was going on with it but I thought perhaps she knew something I didn't.

Claudia had barely moved from behind her desk, but I could hardly sit still. "It's gotten larger. He's now included Warren in it. Roth is including sections of his novel *The Nitpicker*."

"How did that happen?" I asked.

"Warren is hot right now, and Roth likes him," Claudia answered.

I turned and left the office without saying anything. Claudia clearly found my leaving abrupt so she got up and followed me. "Where are you going? You want to have lunch?"

"No," I said, and didn't bother turning to see her reaction.

Once on the street I took out my cell phone and called Sarah. I quickly made a plan with her to meet me that night. She was hesitant but I could hear how anxious she was. I could also hear in her voice that she needed to make our meeting discreet, no doubt because of Warren.

I then called Danni and she quickly answered. "Yes?"

"It's Max Foreman," I said.

"I no longer work for Doug Harris," she responded.

"You can help promote Tom Chillo."

"I'm out of work."

"I can pay you," I told her.

"I spoke with Warren Fabrizi about Tom. I'll fill you in when I see you," she said. "Come to my place tonight."

She gave me an address in Williamsburg, and I told her I'd see her around nine. I needed to see Sarah first but before I did, I spent the afternoon and early evening showing bookstore managers the box set of my novels. Even though I only had a few copies, I thought that if they were displayed, who knew what could happen.

I felt the ticking clock getting closer to that stroke of midnight that loomed only a few days away. I had to do everything I could to take those steps toward my immortality.

Sarah's nose was red when she walked in from the cold, meeting me at Think Coffee on the strange corner of Eighth Avenue by Greenwich Avenue and West Thirteenth Street where four or five streets ran together like an artery gone haywire.

I was in the back sipping a tea. She nodded, then ordered her own tea and in a few minutes she was sitting beside me. She had grown her hair and styled it differently.

"You look good," I told her.

"So do you," she replied.

I noticed that she did seem as if a weight had been lifted from her. I could tell that she knew someone cared about her and she was thriving in that concern. I didn't want to call it love because I was suspicious of Fabrizi's intentions, but Sarah did look in love as well as looking confident in being loved. I was happy for her and glad that we both had found someone right for us. Though once again, I was suspicious of Fabrizi's motivations— and Jennifer wasn't a living human being.

I apologized for not replying to her e-mails or phone calls since my last trip and made up a story about my father dying. She consoled me and then I changed the subject to Tom Chillo. Sarah quickly told me that Warren Fabrizi was now the executor of Tom's work. She also told me the same information about Fabrizi's movie and TV screenplay adaptations that Claudia had mentioned.

"He loves Tom's work. I feel comfortable with all his attention. I felt so good about him that I turned over the title and authority of executor of Tom's estate to Warren," she said.

I tried not to show my outrage. "Tom didn't think much of Warren," I said.

Sarah looked at me suspiciously. "That's so odd."

"What is?"

"Warren said the same thing. But he laughed when he said it. When you talk about Tom, you said it as if you knew him. I mean, as if you *really* knew him. More than I did."

"What did he say to you about Warren?"

Sarah shifted in her chair. She spoke softly yet audibly over the noise that filtered around us. "Tom was always competitive with other writers. He didn't like Warren much but Tom's dead now and Warren cares about me. I know he does." Sarah looked up at me, seemingly wanting to justify her relationship with Fabrizi.

I spent most of that time in the café trying to lean the conversation toward Fabrizi, but Sarah kept leaning back to me. Eventually, I asked her point-blank, "Does Warren know you're here?"

"Of course," she said.

A few minutes later we were walking northwest into the biting wind, away from where I knew Fabrizi had a condo, and toward the Hudson River and New Jersey. "I think of death, Tom's death, a lot. I think of my own, ever since he died. I think of how much I loved him and how much I have to get over it. But when I'm with you, I don't feel sad about any of that. When I'm with you, it's as if I'm with Tom. Why?"

"I don't know," I lied.

"Is it because you really love his work?"

"Perhaps," I said as a gust of wind pressed down on us. I stood in front of her to protect her from the blast. I felt her gloved hand on my chin. I looked down and I saw her brown eyes looking up at me.

"There's so much I want to tell you," she said.

"About?" I asked.

"About Tom," she answered. "I want to tell you how much he cared about writing. I want to tell you how much he cared about storytelling and his characters and how they spoke and what they thought about life and death. And love. He hardly showed these passions in his own life or to the people around him, if you know what I mean."

"Maybe he thought he was in his own way?" I asked.

"You keep defending him. . . . Why?"

I didn't answer. Sarah didn't take her eyes off me. "He lived to write and he was thrilled when his books got published. He enjoyed going to openings and parties, but I know the glamour was never a part of what drove him."

"Do you know what drove him?" I asked, knowing. Or so I thought. I needed to hear it from her.

"I still don't know what made him spend all those hours writing. I really don't know what it was that glued him to the computer screen. I know it was a job, an occupation . . . "

I cut her off. "It's a vocation, not an occupation. It's a *calling*."

I could see she was trembling in the cold but I had to continue.

"We live in mediocre times. When art is now second place to science and technology, when the best artists aren't heard from and those wealthy and connected in the real world, who have all the power to make a difference, prefer to hold high those artists with no back-bones and no true voices," I told her.

"And you know why? Because those artists can be controlled. They are no threat to the status quo!"

"Now you sound like him," Sarah told me. She touched my lips with her gloved hand. "Trust Warren. He will do well for Tom."

"Are you going to him now?" I asked.

"No, I'm going home," she answered.

"You love him, don't you?" I asked, not as Max, but as Tom.

"You can see it?" she said, smiling.

"I can."

We then parted ways at the corner. I had set a plan in motion that came to me all at once, knowing that, as always in life, everything happens at the same time and you just have to know what choice to make that matters most.

I had set out to make Tom Chillo's work important, his sacrifice significant, and his name famous. The only other thing on my mind was Jennifer, my new love, my soul mate in death, and how we were to make love in real life, with flesh-and-blood bodies, to fulfill a thirst and desire that we had discovered for each other in the Afterlife. I was looking forward to that moment more than I had ever looked forward to any moment like it when I was actually alive. How odd my nonexistence was becoming.

I was glad I had seen Sarah, and it was probably for the last time. When she walked away, all those years we had spent together walked away as well—not into the darkness of night but into the future, her future, and hopefully I was walking into a future I had worked so hard for.

I assessed my situation and decided Warren Fabrizi would have to wait. Right now, I needed to see Danni.

CHAPTER 16

anni met me in her slippers, bundled up in a wool cap, gloves, scarf, and heavy sweater, sipping hot tea in a big cup. "No heat," she told me. She was wearing a wool cap and gloves.

Her apartment was on North Eighth Street in Williamsburg near Our Lady of Mount Carmel Church. It was a fifth-floor walkup and the wood floors creaked when I walked into her place.

"The landlord's being a bitch," she said apologetically. Of course, I didn't feel the cold so I smiled and told her not to worry.

We sat on a big sofa as she nearly wrapped her legs around an electric heater. I told her everything I had learned since I had been back and added that I could pay her a few hundred dollars when I was sure I had what I needed from her.

She told me that Doug had fired her but then abruptly quit his blog, moved in with his newly found wealthy male lover, and then they both moved to Europe.

"I didn't know he was gay," I said.

"Oh, I did. Big secret. He thought of himself as bi," she said roughly, making it obvious that she had slept with him, perhaps on more than one occasion.

"Let me take you somewhere for something to eat," I said.

A short while later we were sitting in DuMont on Union Avenue across from Kellogg's Diner. I knew this was the place to have big burgers, which I thought Danni might need considering her no-heat situation, and she did order the burger.

I took a good look at her. She had grown her hair; it fell in soft, blond waves on her shoulders. She seemed less tense than our last encounter, which she brought up. "That was odd of me, last time we were together. I never heard from you but I don't blame you; I came on really strong and people don't see me like that, coming on strong being tiny and a girl," she said all in one long breath.

I smiled. "It was all good. I didn't get back to you because I was dealing with family stuff. But I am back and I'm glad I am if only for a short time." I didn't want to talk about our sexual encounter so I quickly told her what I had learned from both Claudia and Sarah. I also told her about my meeting with Allan Roth, leaving out the part of his knowing about the Writers Afterlife. Then I asked about Fabrizi.

"Warren Fabrizi came to see me," she told me just as her hamburger arrived. I tried to remain patient as she alternated between eating and talking. I looked out the window and I saw it was snowing, large flakes, dazzling the people who were walking by the window.

Just then I looked back to Danni and she sprouted wings, two big ones from each side, flowing up in a spray of white feathers. They exploded outwardly and up, nearly touching the low-lying ceiling. Danni was oblivious to what was happening to her. She kept on eating her burger, her head lowered to her plate, the burger dripping with ketchup, melted cheese oozing through her fingers. I, however, was astonished.

I was sure no one saw what I was seeing; otherwise, there would have been pandemonium in the restaurant. Conversations still continued, people laughed, the candles continued to flicker on the tables, and it seemed no one noticed that the petite, articulate, and very hungry young woman was sitting at my table with enormous angel-like wings.

I pushed the table away from me, got up, walked through the restaurant, and only stopped moving once I'd stepped outside. A few people were huddled in the cold outside the restaurant smoking cigarettes. They hardly glanced at me.

"Tom!" I took a deep breath when I saw Lucy from the Writers Afterlife standing in the middle of the street as cars, trucks, buses, and bicycles drove *through* her. "It's happening," she said to me in a calm voice.

"What?" I asked.

"The two worlds are colliding."

I felt weak in the knees, uncomfortable in Max Foreman's skin. People were walking by on Union Avenue, and snow was falling around me. I felt dizzy.

"Go back," she said. "As your guide in the Writers Afterlife I must warn you. You must go back."

I felt myself breathing heavily as if I were in some kind of chamber. Lucy looked me directly in the eyes. "The worlds are colliding for you, Tom. Ghosts and the dead are going to haunt you, and you may not be strong enough."

"Strong enough?" I asked.

Lucy nodded. Now the light changed to red and people were walking through her. "If you have a breakdown, you will lose sight of your quest."

"But I'm dead, how can I have a breakdown?" I asked.

"How can you be here and how can I be here? Welcome to the Writers Afterlife," she answered. "Your imagination means everything."

"Do you mean I'm imagining all of this?"

Lucy didn't answer. I wanted to reach out to her, but she didn't move in any direction. I focused on her face and looked deeply into her eyes, hoping to find out if I could believe her. I couldn't decide if she was lying to me or warning me.

When I got back to Danni, she hardly knew I'd been absent. She had devoured her burger. I sat down and she looked up at me. "That was really tasty, thanks."

I nodded and tried to remember what she'd been saying right before I saw the wings. "So what did Fabrizi ask you?"

"He wanted to know what I knew about you."

"And you told him *what*?"

Danni smiled. "Just that you were a fan of Tom Chillo's."

I quickly paid the check and walked Danni home. As we strolled through the streets she told me that she would be available for me in my mission to make Tom Chillo a respected author. They were her exact words: "a respected author."

She then smiled and asked, "Can I stay with you? I need someplace with heat."

I felt dizzy again. I felt as if I were being pulled in two opposite directions, two separate worlds. I could see gusts of wind blowing up in a squall down alleyways, up and over rooftops.

I told Danni that she could come with me but then I realized I hadn't bothered to get a hotel room this time. Thankfully, I remembered seeing a motel on Lorimer Street east of the Brooklyn–Queens Expressway. I told Danni to go home and bring some clothes over.

The winter air was nearly pristine. I checked in and was given a room on the top floor facing the Manhattan skyline. I spent the next half hour waiting for Danni, making a plan. I needed to find out where Fabrizi was; I needed to confront him.

"What do you know about Fabrizi?" I asked Danni as soon as she came into my room.

"He is now seeing Chillo's old girlfriend, Sarah," she said, nestling in, getting cozy. Before I could react, she was kissing Max Foreman.

I wanted to stop her but at the same time I did need her help.

"I really like you," she said as I stepped back, her arms draped around my shoulders.

"I like you also," I told her with Max's best congenial Canadian manner.

She began to remove her clothing when I looked at my watch.

"Do you have to be somewhere?" she asked.

"Yes. Sarah said she was going to be home, so perhaps I can go see Fabrizi."

"Do you want me to come with you?" Danni asked.

"Nope. I'm fine."

She then curled up on the bed. "I'll be here waiting for you when you get back. Wake me when you do, Max," she said.

I nodded that I would, then left the motel. In seconds I transported myself to the Meatpacking District and stood outside Fabrizi's condo.

I looked up to the second floor and I saw the living room light was on. Fabrizi was on the phone pacing as he spoke. He had a lot of energy and always seemed to be moving either by walking or moving his hands or his head.

I stood in the sharp wind coming off the Hudson River and I had an idea that I should try the unthinkable. My inspiration for the unthinkable came from another writer, and that writer was Poe. I concentrated on turning myself back into who I really was. In a matter of seconds I became Tom Chillo once again. Then I dialed Fabrizi's cell phone. I watched as he got my call.

"Hello?"

I could see that he hadn't recognized the incoming number. "Warren, it's me, Tom."

"Tom who?" he asked.

"Tom Chillo," I said.

I saw the silence as he froze. Before he could react I continued, "I hear you want to make a movie and a TV series out of my novels."

"Who is this?" he said sharply, trying to play the tough guy.

"It's Tom, pal."

"This is a sick joke because Tom Chillo is dead."

"Come to the window," I told him.

I moved into the light thrown against the side of the building from a lamppost. I looked up, watching Fabrizi hesitate as he slowly made his way to the window. He looked down at me. Just by his reaction I knew he was looking at Tom Chillo, the long-dead-and-buried Tom Chillo.

Fabrizi pushed his face up against his window. He lowered the phone. I didn't move. I just stared at him. I lifted my cell. He saw me do it. Then he returned his cell to his ear.

"Come down now and we will talk," I said.

CHAPTER 17

Warren Fabrizi and I were sitting face-to-face across a table in a small, nearly empty coffee shop right off Jane Street.

I sipped coffee, facing a very tired-looking Fabrizi and the large window, watching passersby while listening to the waiter and manager talk to each other in Spanish.

"This is the same coffee shop Christina Mendez comes to when looking for her husband, Jorge. You know why? He'd worked here," I said, looking around and enjoying the memory of being inspired.

"What are you talking about?" Warren asked.

"My second novel: *The Dead Mexican*. Christina Mendez comes here because Jorge had worked here when he first came to New York City," I said. "Aren't you putting that scene in the screenplay?"

"This is impossible," Warren told me. He put his head down on the table for a moment, raised it again then looked directly at me. "I'm having a conversation with a dead man."

"Nothing after death is impossible," I replied.

"But you're not really here, are you?"

"I certainly am here."

He squirmed in his chair, not sure of where to look.

"You should talk Allan Roth into publishing excerpts from my novels," I said.

"So, you're not really dead, are you?" he said calmly but with an air of inquisitiveness.

I grinned. "Oh, I'm dead, all right."

"And you're sitting here with me?"

"I am."

"Talking about your novel."

"That's correct."

"How is that possible?"

"Just go with it for now," I answered.

He pondered what I told him and then he continued, "Okay, so tell me, who is Max Foreman?"

"Someone I created to help Tom Chillo."

"This guy who has met with Sarah and everyone else isn't a real person?"

"Exactly."

"Wow."

"Oh, and I am glad you are going to make a movie and a TV series out of my novels."

Fabrizi squinted and nodded. "They're good novels. I know I can do a good job adapting them."

I was a little taken aback by the sound of sincerity in his voice. Now I wondered if Fabrizi truly did admire my novels after all.

I sat back. I had expected my antagonist to battle me with some fierce maliciousness, some maniacal ranting, some vicious and condescending comments about me, Tom, but he was saying nothing of the sort. Instead, he acted perplexed and was seemingly working on projects that connected the two of us. Now I was confused, too.

"I hear you're seeing Sarah," I said without inflection.

"Yes. I always found her lovely. When Tom died—"

"I'm Tom," I interrupted.

"Right. Well, when *you* died she called me about your work and asked me to consider becoming your executor. Eventually, I agreed. We spent some time together and the next thing we were doing was seeing each other," he told me. "Do you find that odd?"

"What do you think I would think?" I asked.

"You're dead. It never would have happened if you hadn't died, so the question is irrelevant," Fabrizi responded.

"Nothing is irrelevant, Warren, including what the dead think or feel."

A few minutes later we were back on the street, Fabrizi cold and fatigued and I energized with a mission that I only had a few more days' time to pull off.

"You believe you are, were, a great writer?" Fabrizi asked through clenched teeth as the wind blew harder.

"Yes."

"What makes a great writer?" he continued.

"What makes a writer great? An extraordinary use of language. The ability to tell a story. Creating memorable characters. Dedication to learning the craft. Having a substantial audience. Critics can make some writers famous, yet the biggest test of all is time and how deep the writer's well of imagination is," I told him.

"Textbook answer," he replied.

Despite Fabrizi's accurate assessment, I held back the truth, which was that some writers made themselves great by going back into life and forcing the world to reassess them or just to accept who they had been all along.

"What do *you* think makes a writer great?" I asked.

"Talent and luck," he answered.

"Are you a great writer?" I asked.

"No," he answered. "I'm no genius. And I don't know if you are, *were*, either."

"What makes a writer famous?" I then asked.

Fabrizi took his time answering that question. "All that you said previously, but also one other thing," he said.

"And what is that?" I asked.

"The unknowable," he said.

"Bullshit. Get my work in Roth's anthology."

"I refuse to be intimidated by a ghost." He reached out and jabbed me, hoping to get a reaction.

I just grinned. "What, you think your hand would go through me? I'm flesh and blood, Warren!"

"That's scientifically impossible!" he shouted.

"Screw science. We're writers. We live, thrive, and endure because of our imaginations. Use yours, for God's sake!"

I left Warren and walked into the night, thinking of Jennifer. I wanted to see her right then but I knew that it was impossible. I had to keep to my plan and she had to keep to hers. I had to work my magic, she had to work hers, and then we would enjoy one last night as flesh-and-blood lovers.

CHAPTER 18

Allan Roth was doing what he always did late at night in his Upper West Side apartment: reading. He was an insomniac with large, dark bags under his eyes. He was sitting on a large sofa in the dim light of his den. Two night tables stood on either side of the sofa. One held a reading lamp, the other his cocktail of scotch and club soda. He wore a dark blue robe, big rimmed reading glasses, and black slippers. The thin strands of hair on his head were combed back. He looked more like an eighteenth-century critic than a twenty-first-century one.

I stood as Tom Chillo to his side, out of the glare of the reading lamp. Roth's den was a library with book-cases on all four walls. He read with such intensity it took him a while before he looked and saw me standing there. He jumped, knocked over his drink, and tried to get to his feet, but his belly was so round that gravity kept him immobile.

"Relax, I'm not going to hurt you," I said to him.

He continued to move around in his seat, squirming to get up. I went over to him, put my arms on his shoulders, and pressed him back down into the sofa.

He looked up at me. I could see his eyes through his thick-rimmed reading glasses.

He steadied himself. "Who are you?" he asked.

"Tom Chillo. The last time we met I was Max Foreman. If we meet again, I might come back as your dead mother."

He looked unnerved. "Please don't come back as my dead mother."

"I want you to publish excerpts from my two novels."

"Which novels?"

"*The Last Vision* and *The Dead Mexican*."

"I don't know them," he whimpered.

"Then read them!"

He cowered. "Of course." He got up and walked to a bookcase. I noticed that he'd alphabetized his books by author. He searched under *C*, then slowly turned to me. "I don't have them."

"Then get them on Amazon."

"Of course."

"And by the way, Warren Fabrizi is going to come to you to suggest you include my work in your anthology. That will be how everyone will know you included it. That will be the official story."

I sat. He sat. Here was my biggest enemy and potentially my biggest ally. I suddenly realized that throughout my career I'd had to deal with people I didn't like to get what I truly loved.

"I'm a great writer," I said without hesitation.

"Of course you are. But can you explain to me how you know this?"

"All my life people told me I was."

"All my life people told *me* that I was interesting. I don't even know what it means to be interesting. However, I also don't take what other people say seriously."

I stood. "Don't humor me. I'm great. I belong with the Eternals."

"In the Writers Afterlife."

"Yes. I don't belong in the Valley of Those on the Verge."

"And you are there now?"

"Yes."

I could see him relaxing. "Are you here now in my apartment for my educated literary opinion of your work or are you here to threaten me?" he asked with authority.

"Both," I shot back.

"Of course. Well, I don't know your work. I do know contemporaries of yours like Kenneth Ungly. Now, the *New York Times* critics always give him good reviews. That said, it's hard for other critics to attack him. So, even if I believe he is overrated, I won't go against the grain," he told me.

"You seem very relaxed."

"I am."

"Even though you're speaking to a dead man?"

"A dead man who seems quite reasonable," he said.

"I want you to be my Samuel Johnson," I said.

"You can't compare yourself with Shakespeare."

"I'm not comparing. I'm saying that I deserve the fame for my work. I died young but what I wrote up to that point is good. *Very* good," I said.

"Fortysomething is not young. Keats's death at twenty-six was young. Shelley's death at twenty-nine was young. You did not die young so please do not perpetuate that falsity anymore."

I felt the skin on my forehead tighten.

"I wish I knew your work but in all honesty, I prefer more sophisticated writing. I prefer those who come from the middle class at the very least," Roth said. "I prefer Harold Pinter and Samuel Beckett over Henry Miller and Clifford Odets."

"So, it's a matter of taste?"

"Quality."

"Prejudice."

"And educated judgment."

"Do you like Wilson?"

"Which one? Lanford or August?"

"August."

"Sorry, no."

I realized then that I was fighting a mountain of indifference, not just with Roth but with all literary critics of my era.

I walked closer to Roth and stood over him. I opened my hand. I was going to have to be more like Poe than Shakespeare in my quest for fame. I had to see Roth more as Rufus Griswold than Samuel Johnson.

With my open palm I smacked Roth across the face. It gave me an ocean of pleasure to see his reading glasses fly off, his cheek go red, his eyes glare in pain, and his mouth drop. "I don't give a rat's ass what you think of my work, you vile, bigoted old man. I will torture you with a smack every week for the rest of your life if you don't praise my work in your new anthology, do you understand?" I said calmly.

He nodded.

I leaned in and smacked him on the other side of the face, this time with the back of my hand. He yelped. I grinned. Naturally, I wouldn't be able to smack him in the face every week for the rest of his life because this was my last entry into life from the dead. I just hoped his fear of my returning would motivate him.

"You just got bitch-slapped, sir," I told him. "Bitch-slapped by a ghost."

Roth's big eyes looked up at me. He smiled.

"What?" I asked sternly.

Then his face crumbled. "It's not fair," he said. He started to say something else but then moaned, "What does everyone want from me? It's not fair."

"What's not fair?"

"Look at me!" he shouted, then walked toward his bookshelves, throwing his arms up. "It's the middle of the night and what am I doing? Reading! What kind of life is this? I'm surrounded by books. And no one cares about books anymore! I love holding books, opening the covers, turning pages. Now there are e-books and Kindles and all that other nonsense."

This reaction was not what I expected.

"No one is here but you and you're not even real. You're a ghost. I want a human being in my life," he said.

I was perplexed. He came slowly toward me with tears in his eyes. "I'm lonely," he said.

"Excuse me?"

He came right to my face and leaned against my chest. He put his arms around me. "Hold me."

"Huh?" I didn't move. He put his arms around me and held me closely, snuggling his face into my chest right below my chin. Then he slowly dropped his hands down both sides of my back, pulling me closer. "I'll help you with your book, I will."

I still didn't move. He then grabbed my ass with his right hand. I jumped back and saw those big eyes looking back at me.

"I'm not unattractive, Tom," he said softly.

I watched him in the dim light. I grimaced. "What the hell are you talking about?"

"I'm taking about human fragility and solitude. This could be such a private moment between us. Who would believe an indiscretion between a middle-aged academic and a ghost? I will be discreet. You can count on that."

I shook my head. "This isn't me."

"What isn't? An attraction between two people?"

"This is not an attraction and it's not between two people. As you just said, I'm dead."

He squeezed my arm. "You feel real to me." And with that, he came up to my face to kiss me.

I felt the soft surface of his lips on mine for a second. I shoved him back and he fell against a bookcase.

"Roth! Enough!"

He managed to keep his balance and then unleashed all his fury on me. "You idiot! I could have helped you. I could have done something for you. Instead, in your own simple arrogance you think you're too good for me. You're too . . . what? Handsome? Look in the mirror, Chillo!"

I frowned. I had no idea what was happening anymore. My fundamental reason for coming to see him was now eroding and transforming into something else entirely that I had not anticipated. Roth was a human being.

"I can't do this," I said.

"Then get out! Get out!"

I stood there in his library, more confused than ever. I nodded, then turned and walked to the door. I heard him gently sobbing behind me.

"It could have been lovely," he whimpered. "Go, please."

So I did.

———

Out on the street I felt the tremendous crush of disappointment. I had failed in my mission and now I had no idea what to do. I looked up at the light in his window. It was still on.

I stood there in the night feeling creeped out and annoyed with myself. Yes, I'd been thrown off-balance by his proposal but at the same time I could have handled it better, been more magnanimous and more understanding instead of belligerent and demeaning. I mean, his offer of putting me in the anthology might have been his way of asking for comfort, some conversation, perhaps keeping him company.

But I was being naïve. I knew better though I was pretending not to. My denial was being driven by my own ruthless ambition. I was no babe in the woods; I knew that the very notion of sleeping with someone to make you famous was not only ill-advised but also unlikely to work out. It often led to humiliation and disappointment—unless, of course, you liked the person. I didn't like Allan Roth the person and certainly not in that way.

I wondered if Roth had been a woman the same age and physical bearing as Roth the man, would it have been possible for me, Tom Chillo, to have sex with her for potential favors? I quickly dismissed that notion, as an arrangement like that would become very complicated. A female Roth might eventually want something more than I'd have any intention of giving. Resentments would build and before you knew it, we'd become fierce enemies.

Who knew the adventures of a dead writer could be filled with so much drama, turmoil, and perplexing clashes of incongruity?

I decided I should apologize. I knew I was tempting fate by going back to see Roth, but at the same time he deserved an apology. I rang his bell but nothing happened. I wanted to properly enter through the front door so I rang the bell again and waited, but again there was no answer. So I transported myself inside his apartment, and there he was lying on his back in the middle of the living room.

Roth's mouth and eyes were wide open and his right hand was gripping his left side. Though I was no medical expert, it seemed that Allan Roth had just died of a heart attack.

CHAPTER 19

Lucy appeared to me somewhere between night and dawn. "I'm sorry, Tom."

"So, I only have Fabrizi to push now," I told her.

"Your time is running out," she told me, then disappeared.

I was suddenly alone and found myself drifting between life and the Afterlife. I walked along the frozen parts of the East River close to the shore on the Brooklyn and Queens side so I could get a good look at the Manhattan skyline. I wasn't going to see it anymore, and that thought made me a little numb even though I was dead and wasn't supposed to feel anything. Oddly, when I died it happened so quickly I hadn't realized I wouldn't see the skyline anymore, so I didn't think I'd miss it.

As the cold wind blew sharply from the north, pushing into my face and occasionally obstructing my vision, I thought of all the things in life that I missed. I missed change, laughter, talking to other people about shared experiences that had nothing to do with being writers. I missed fearing death. I realized the big difference between fear and anxiety. I felt extreme anxiety in the Valley but I had no fear.

Death itself, it turned out, was actually nothing to fear. Dying wasn't a bad thing. Living with life's profound mysteries was, however, very difficult.

It was then that I bumped into him. He was right there in front of me, drifting along the streets, looking haggard and half-dead, mumbling to himself. Though he was in the wrong city, he was in my imagination after all. It was Jared Gray, the poet and hero of my novel *The Last Vision*.

"Jared," I said.

He turned to me. There he was, his long hair flowing over his ears, his handsome features now crumbling thanks to years of hard drinking, drugs, and long nights without sleep.

"I love everything," he told me. "Even the loneliness that hits me like a brick wall."

I wasn't sure of the time, but as I'd created him and written the novel, I knew he would die at midnight by throwing himself in front of a Long Island Rail Road train on the Port Jefferson line: The 11:18, to be exact, right outside Port Jefferson proper.

He mumbled to himself, struggling to complete the poem, and with each line he had a new insight into the meaning of his own life. His brown eyes had lost all their fire and he was now done for, but at the same time close to a victory he had struggled to attain all his life: a worthy poem.

Without saying another word, he staggered into the darkness.

In the middle of this disorientation I found myself standing over Warren Fabrizi's bed. When he opened his eyes, I picked him up and carried him over to the open window. I shoved his head into the freezing cold as Warren panicked and struggled.

"Allan Roth died of a heart attack last night. That only leaves you, my friend. You! Only you can help me now," I told him.

Then I shoved Warren across the room. He was barefoot, wearing sweatpants and a T-shirt. He fell on his shoulder and groaned. "That hurt," he said.

I walked over to him, picked him up by his collar, and tossed him onto the bed. He groaned again but this time he didn't say anything. I looked around the room and spotted his laptop on the desk. "Start writing!" I shouted.

He made his way to his desk and turned on his computer. "What do you want me to write?"

"I want you write that I am the most interesting writer you ever read. I want you to compare me with all the great writers," I said.

"Do you want to dictate exactly what you want me to write?"

I inched closer to him. "Warren, I've been *there*."

He looked unblinkingly at me.

"I've been to the Writers Afterlife. I've been to where the Eternals are. I've personally met Shakespeare, Emily Brontë, Melville, Wilde, and other celebrated dead writers. And they are happy, Warren. *Happy!* They will live in eternal bliss for the rest of eternity because they are famous," I said. "They interact with their characters, they beam with glory, and they shine with eternal fame. They will never suffer ever again in all eternity because they are legends!"

Warren was riveted by what I had to say. His eyes were glued to me.

"They are celebrated, illustrious, recognized, eminent, and renowned in the Afterlife for all time," I said. Energy was shooting through my every fiber. I felt the ticking clock and knew my time in life was dwindling.

Warren sighed and said, "Wow."

"And I want *that*."

Warren relaxed. He believed me. "And where are you now in this Writers Afterlife?"

"I am in the Valley of Those on the Verge. I am waiting, like many thousands of other writers, for the call from the living that I made it. When that happens, I can join the Eternals," I said.

"So that means if you aren't famous when you die, you have to wait. And you can wait forever," he stated.

"Exactly. And I was given one week to come here back to life to change things if I can. So far, I've hit nothing but roadblocks."

"Do you feel pain in this valley?" Warren was clearly more interested in the world I was now a part of than what I had to say about myself in life.

"The pain of anxiety. There's no need for sleep or food, but you do *feel* and have all kinds of emotions," I answered.

Warren stood. He was seemingly free of all fear of me. "I'm not a great writer, Tom. If I died, I'd go to the Valley and stay there the rest of eternity, that's for certain. I don't like the way that place sounds. I'm a showrunner on a TV show now. Do they have showrunners in with the Eternals?"

"How can there be? You know that TV is written by committee. The Eternals wrote their own stuff, created their own characters, and took great leaps of faith about their own worth. No writer or creator of a TV show belongs up there!" I said vehemently.

Warren was now growing pensive. "I'm in love with Sarah. I always have been," he confessed. "Now that I'm with her, I want to stay with her. We are talking about adopting."

"Seriously?"

"Yes," Warren answered firmly.

"Okay, that's good for you."

"I'll be honest with you. I did want to destroy your career. I did want to bury your reputation. And yes, I was jealous of you all those years despite my own success. But when you died, it all changed. I was able to see Sarah and I realized how much I was in love with her. I had realized that my dislike for you was based on the fact that you had her and I didn't," he said.

I was taken aback. Warren really did love Sarah and he was telling me the truth. "Being with her made me see you differently. Once I was secure that we were really a couple and she no longer really cared about you, I was free! Free!" Warren was now walking around the room. "I had no underlying intentions about your work, meaning producing and writing the adaptations, other than seeing them as a way to make a living for Sarah and me. Your novels will translate well to film and TV. I want them to provide for her and our future child."

I was stymied because I realized that Warren was no longer my natural enemy. He was just another writer in the pool of writers and was not standing in my way in my pursuit of eternal fame. "So, you see my work as a bank."

"Yes!" Just then I could see something occur to Warren. "You said something when we were at the coffee shop, about that being the place where you thought Jorge worked when he came to New York City, right?"

"Yeah, I used that place in my mind. It made it easier for me to write the scene when Christina goes there to ask about her husband."

"Give me more about Christina Mendez. Stuff you didn't put in the novel. Scenes, thoughts, insights about her and the story that you left out, but were good. You know that happens to us all the time. The stuff we leave out of a story is sometimes very compelling."

I listened closely.

Warren saw that I knew what he was getting at. "I want to put those scenes in the screenplay adaptation. I want the great stuff that never made it into the book. I have the author standing right in front of me now! This is great, Tom, great. I want you do the same thing for *The Last Vision*, too. I need more material because it's a cable series."

"I just ran into Jared Gray on the street before, actually," I said.

"What?"

"He was mumbling to himself and said, 'I love everything, even the loneliness that hits me like a brick wall.'"

"That line is not in the book," Warren told me.

"Yeah, I know. How could it be, he just said it to me."

Warren smiled and shook his head at the same time. "Okay, this is amazing stuff."

It happened just like that. The two of us working for hours and hours, deep into the night and into the next day, Warren without sleep, I opening up like a damn bursting with ideas, notions still in my brain but never used, all for the adaptations of my two novels, all gifts to Warren and Sarah, all to make a great movie and a great cable series. I owed Sarah that much.

Sometime the following night, as Warren sat half-asleep in his chair in front of the computer and I reveled in being able to have one more creative outburst, I said good-bye to him and left. I found myself wandering through the streets. I had so little to drive me now. And I understood Warren. He chose life and its comforting

aspects over immortality. When faced with his own loneliness he opted for affection, care, and love. Long ago, I'd
decided to pick the pursuit of greatness over love. The
point, though, was: What *is* greatness? Drive, talent,
luck? The combination of all three? I was dead and still
didn't know the answer.

CHAPTER 20

I was hallucinating more and more during the time that remained of my journey back into life. It was as if my DNA were breaking down and I was becoming a fragment of a human being. I found it arduous to stay focused. I called out to Lucy and she appeared to me in the middle of Times Square.

"Can you help me?" I asked.

"Come back to the Afterlife and you'll be fine," she said sympathetically.

"I can't go yet. I promised to see Jennifer," I replied.

"Tom, you are breaking apart. Your neurons and protons and molecules are disintegrating rapidly. You might not make the entire prearranged time allotment back here in life," she said.

"Is that normal?" I asked her.

"Not always. As you broke the week up into two parts, two halves, it might be a reaction to that," she told me.

I wasn't sure if any of the tourists could see her as distinctly as I could. But there she was in her sparkly ballerina outfit, standing in the center of Times Square in the blinding cold wind as dusk fell like a heavy mountain through the thick New York City winter air.

"I need to prevail!" I shouted.

I saw her smile to me warmly like Glinda the Good Witch, waving good-bye, fading into the light. "Safe journey back, Tom Chillo," she said, and then she was gone.

—⁓—

Jennifer told me that we should meet on the corner of Mott and Spring Streets at 10 p.m. so I drifted downtown without any sense of nostalgia or sorrow in saying good-bye to the world.

There was no one else I wanted to see anymore. The only entity I was hoping to spend time with was Jennifer and though she was long dead, I would see her as she was when alive and that was something that I anticipated with longing and joy. I wondered what she had been up to and how she was doing on her own pursuit of immortality.

I was hoping she would be able to see me before our appointed hour because for the first time since I had died, time itself seemed to have a value and that worth created an emotion in me.

This time, *time* was my enemy because I was going to run out of it; it would no longer feed me the essential thing I needed to make my work known. This time I was really dying. The first time I died was only a prequel. This new death, my third death, was the final one. This was the true death. This death was the one that mattered. This was the death for all perpetuity.

I found a small park on Bleecker Street and Sixth Avenue named after a priest, Father Demo. I sat in the cold thinking about my plight and concentrating on seeing Jennifer, my love. A stranger sat beside me. I didn't take much notice of him until he looked at me with hypnotic hazel eyes. He was young with excellent features perfectly set in his soft, pale face. He had brown hair that was swept over a widow's peak. He grinned at me.

"I'm Allan Roth," he said in a melodious voice so unlike Allan Roth's. "I've come back from the Writers Afterlife. It seems that I'm not famous as of yet so I am residing in the Valley of Those on the Verge. I took the opportunity to visit life to make sure that my anthology places me in the realm of the famous. How are you doing, Tom Chillo?"

I wasn't just stunned; I was mortified, horrified, and helpless all at once.

"You murdered me, Chillo, and now I have nothing on my mind but revenge." Despite the soft voice I could hear Roth's malicious intent spewing out of the young man's full lips.

I wanted to defend myself but I already unintentionally killed Roth. I hadn't murdered him when he was alive and now I couldn't murder him; he was already dead.

"For my revenge I've destroyed the only other thing that matters to you other than your fame and that is your love for Jennifer." He grinned again.

"What did you do?" I was hysterical now.

"I made a deal with your precious Jennifer to assure her chances of immortality by *destroying* yours."

"How did you do that?"

"I introduced her to Stephan Bears, a good friend. He is editing an anthology of the most influential Asian American female writers. She persuaded him just last night to name her the forerunner to Amy Tan, Gish Jen, and Iris Chang."

"How did she do that?"

"By seducing him. Fucking his brains out in ways he had never experienced before or ever will again. Stephan is a very seducible man without any moral backbone. And he's married, so Jennifer coming into his life, if only briefly, made a major impact on his existence."

The image of my Jennifer having sex with another man crushed me. I didn't want to hear anymore.

"And there's more." Roth leaned in. "Stephan is my replacement on editing the anthology of contemporary American fiction writers. And you won't be in it."

I was seething.

"He is doing this because it was part of his deal with Jennifer."

"Why did Jennifer make this deal?"

"Because she was afraid you were getting close to being allowed into the land of the Eternals and she wanted to stop you from taking her place."

I cringed. My head was swimming with self-accusation. I had done exactly what I warned myself not to do. I had fallen in love. Worse, I had fallen in love with a writer. Worst of all, I had allowed my feelings to take me away from my goal of being famous. I had never done this in life but now, in death, I had broken this cardinal rule.

Jennifer betrayed me. Her need for immortality made her more ruthless than I ever imagined. I was an idiot for letting my guard down. I wondered if Jennifer had this plan in mind all along or if it was something that occurred spontaneously.

I was mortified as I sat quietly in the chilly wind. Life wasn't the only struggle; death was just as strenuous and filled with just as much pain.

"This isn't over between us, Roth!" I shouted, ignoring the curious glances from passersby.

"Oh, it's over Chillo. You lost! You are condemned to spending the rest of your rotten existence in the Valley of Those on the Verge."

Roth left me alone and all I could do was cry out "Jennifer, why?" but my words just dissolved in the cold wind.

———

I walked aimlessly through the night as my life ticked away. I thought of those lines by the poet Dante Gabriel Rossetti: "From perfect grief there need not be / Wisdom or even memory."

I was an artist uncomfortable with everything other than what I created. Specifically, I was a writer, observer of human behavior, human needs, fears, and suffering. I observed joy and happiness and did my best to experience it, but most important, I did it all by creating characters who were supposed to be as real as I was.

In those final seconds before midnight I recall seeing my reflection in a big window on Sixth Avenue. I thought about how human I was, how flawed. I was anticipating my DNA to implode because this was my final foray into life, and yet the end was anticlimactic.

I looked up the avenue at all the wondrous lights, the faces rushing by, and voices trailing off, and then I quickly looked to where my reflection had been in the window, but it was no longer there and neither was I.

CHAPTER 21

His name was Robert Comb. He was an abstract painter and he had just died at the age of ninety-five. He had lived in a small town in west Kansas and his work had been compared with Jackson Pollock's. "I created the *drip* style of painting!" he told me. "Pollock lived in New York City and he married well; his wife knew the right critics so he got the credit first. But everyone in Kansas who cared *knew* that I created that style a year before he did, but no one recorded it. No one came to my farm house and filmed me dripping the paint on my canvas, so they called me 'Comb the Copycat.' The critic Robert Hughes eventually got to like my work. But even his touting me didn't do me any good. It was too late. I missed the boat. Am I famous?" he asked me.

I was his guide. He had just entered the Valley of Those on the Verge for painters. I explained it all to him about what to expect the same way Joe had explained to me when I first entered this world. Robert was my third case and so far the most memorable. He had decided to be his favorite age, forty-five, in the Afterlife. He had thick dirty-blond hair and though he was short, he had the look of a man who did manual labor. His accent certainly sounded midwestern.

I took him where the Eternals dwelled, and we saw the great painters from the Renaissance and modern times. We saw Michelangelo, Leonardo da Vinci, Caravaggio, Pierre-Auguste Renoir, Claude Monet, William Turner, Edward Hopper. All of them were busy painting. I was amazed by how dedicated they still were to their art even though they didn't have to prove themselves or even paint anymore.

I don't know how long I stayed with Robert, but he was a cantankerous man seriously annoyed and disappointed with his life and career. He had married and had four children and he blamed his lack of recognition on deciding to have a family.

"I should have gone to New York. That was the scene. It was in New York where the galleries were. New York was the place to be. I wanted to walk down that road off my farm and take the bus with nothing but a dollar and bus fare in my pocket. I should have walked out of that marriage and left them to take care of themselves. They never gave a damn about my work. I should have gone to New York and I would have been the next Man Ray or better yet, Pollock died when? When he was forty-five or something stupid like that, right? I lived a half century longer than him. I could have taken his place! Do you know the most I ever sold a painting for was twenty-five grand? Now, despite how prolific I was, I'm lucky if I can get ten grand for a painting," he told me. "What does *his* work go for? Millions, right?" He then stopped as if the answer pained him. We were on a flat bed of grass near a cornfield. This was his imagination, so the world looked exactly how he wanted it to.

"Is Pollock up there where the Eternals are?" he asked.

"He is. Do you want to meet him?"

"Meet him? Like *in person*?"

"Yes."

Robert struggled with the notion. I could see he desperately wanted to meet his nemesis but in the end, he decided against it. "I don't think so," he mumbled. "But . . . "

"But?" I asked.

"I would meet him if there was a way I could change places with him."

"Change places?"

"Take his fame from him. If I could be famous and he wouldn't be anymore."

"I never heard of that happening," I said.

"Oh," he replied with a sigh.

———

As we walked on he continued to gripe about his choosing family and love of his wife over his career. I couldn't hold back anymore. I did the one thing a guide wasn't supposed to do: I interjected my own feelings into the relationship with the deceased.

"Robert, get over it, okay? You loved your kids. You loved your wife. You liked your little town in nowhere Kansas. You didn't go to New York City and become famous because you didn't have the guts. You were afraid of failing. You were afraid of success. You were afraid of changing. You liked being a big fish in a little pond. You were afraid of going to New York only to find yourself a little fish in a very big sea," I told him. "You enjoy complaining because you are safe from all the attacks you would have had to bear if you had been in the spotlight."

I imagine that I hit a nerve because Robert grew quiet for the rest of our walk.

———

With little left to do I escorted the recently deceased Robert Comb to the Valley of Those on the Verge and explained what that meant for him. Just as the last words flew from my lips, he let out a moan. "Don't send me there! Please! I have lived nearly a century waiting and waiting. I cannot wait anymore," he said, his eyes begging me not to leave him alone.

But I had to and I did, allowing his voice to trail off behind me as he disappeared from my view. I glanced back and saw him standing there where I had left him, frozen, looking down into the Valley. I knew he'd eventually take the steps down into eternal oblivion. Despite his protests, he was used to disappointment.

I returned to the Valley of Those on the Verge for writers and did nothing for a while. I tried once to see Jennifer but I couldn't find her. Then one day, she appeared to me.

"I'm leaving," she said flatly.

"Well, whatever you did, you got what you wanted," I said.

"I'm not going to dwell with the Eternals," she told me.

"But you got into the anthology."

"I did and after that they republished my novels but the problem was, the reviewers called them 'dated' and 'old-fashioned,'" she said.

"So, where are you going?"

"Where the normal people go when they die, Tom." She sighed. "I give up."

Without a good-bye kiss or even a handshake, Jennifer turned and walked away, disappearing into the bright sunlight of my imagination.

Nothing much anymore happened in the Valley, though I did hear a name called. It was Sir Thomas Browne. He died on his seventy-seventh birthday in 1682. He was a doctor who wrote about science and the world of nature. His best-known work was something called *Urne-Burial.* I had never heard of him but the talk was that he was a profound influence on many of the Eternals including Johnson, Kafka, Melville, and Samuel Coleridge. Dickinson wrote that she kept his books near her bed. Browne himself, while alive, admitted he was influenced by Michel de Montaigne and believed in witches. It also seemed that he was a devout Christian and believed that living a good life and going to heaven was more important than his everlasting literary fame. It wasn't surprising that I had never heard of him while alive, because most serious contemporary writers hadn't either.

Oddly, two scholars back in life, a husband-and-wife team who had written a best-selling book on Lucretius that brought him into the land where the Eternals dwelled, had now written an important book on Browne. The literary world was expecting that it would make readers take another look at Thomas Browne and perhaps put him in the ranks of the very great. They were already anticipating his fame.

But there was another irony at hand. Those in life had no idea what went on in writers' minds. You see, when his name was called, Browne didn't appear because he wasn't in the Valley. Immediately after his death Browne decided that spending eternity in the Writers Afterlife, much less in the Valley of Those on the Verge, was not for him. "I don't care what eternity thinks of my work. I only care what God thinks about how I lived my life," he'd said. Right after his death in 1682, he joined the rest of ordinary, deceased humanity.

Existence in the Writers Afterlife is not so terrible. Just as life is a mystery, so is the existence that follows. My days are made up of cool breezes and sunny skies, and walks through sensually designed, magnificent cities created in my imagination. I spend hours alongside rivers and lakes as blue as the eyes of a woman from Odessa. At night, I look up at the sky and it's as glorious as any Milky Way galaxy, with the moon and stars as bright and alluring as I'd like them to be.

Yet underneath it all is the perennial anxiety of waiting. Joe didn't lie about that. I waited for my name to be called but then something magnificent happened. A town car came for me. It pulled up to me and just sat there. I waited and watched when a cop, the writer cop I had met some time ago, Timmy Nolan, got out.

He looked at me then said, "They're late." He looked up as if waiting for something.

"Who's late? What are you talking about?" I asked.

Just then I heard my name called. "Tom Chillo!"

Nolan looked at me. "Get in, Mr. Chillo. I'm driving you to where the Eternals dwell."

I was flabbergasted. I couldn't breathe. I was sure it was a ruse and I was being punked. I looked around and we were alone so I got into the backseat. Nolan got behind the wheel and drove up a long, beautiful road lined with hundreds of tall trees and beautiful flowers.

There was a large-screen TV in front of me. It played and both Joe and Lucy were there on-screen in a studio looking directly at me.

"Congratulations, Tom, you made it." Lucy smiled.

"Nice seeing you," Joe said matter-of-factly. "I know you have been too depressed to notice, but it seems that the movie of your novel *The Dead Mexican* won an Oscar for Best Picture. Warren Fabrizi garnered an Oscar nomination for the screenplay adaptation."

Lucy then chimed in. "Because of all the attention you are getting and because you died when you did, everyone is doing stories on you. They believe it's a real human-interest story. Your agent, Claudia Wilson, has been inundated with offers for your stage plays as well. She is now selling the movie rights to *The Borough Chronicles* and there is talk of bringing it to Broadway."

"Oh, and you should see this," Joe stated. A YouTube video appeared of a pretty young woman reading an excerpt of *The Dead Mexican*. It had received over 150 million hits worldwide. The book started selling like crazy. I immediately recognized the young woman as Danni.

Of course, the reason for all this was that Danni did the reading sitting in a chair, in her apartment, *topless*. Yes, topless. I don't know why she did it but the excerpt she chose was wonderful, and despite her being topless it wasn't a distraction. In fact, her performance heightened the effect of the passage.

Danni was giving online interviews and sending out messages to Max Foreman hoping to see him again. I realized she was smitten with him or perhaps even in love. Whatever the reason she did the video, I was eternally grateful. I was actually grateful for Sarah and Warren and Claudia. They had done well for me.

The screen went dark and I sat back looking into the sun as Nolan drove up and into the land where the Eternals dwell. He then stopped the car, got out, and opened my door.

"We're here," he told me.

I got out. I looked around. Everything was beautiful.

"I can't drive any closer."

Nolan then looked at me in a way no one had ever looked at me before. "You're one of them now," he said.

I was humbled.

Nolan then climbed into the car and drove back down the hill.

I was alone and allowed myself to embrace all that had happened to me in my entire life, good and bad, before this moment. I then took a few confident steps into the sunlight.

I heard voices as I walked up the hill. The first two people I saw were Molière and Albert Camus, my long-time favorite writers and thinkers. They were in a café along the Seine; Molière was dressed as if in a performance of *Don Juan* and Camus was just sitting in his chair, leaning back with a cigarette dangling from his lips. He grinned at me and Molière tipped his large yellow hat and also grinned.

A very tiny lady took my arm and led me farther up the hill. I knew immediately it was Carson McCullers. "Lovely day for entering the land of the Eternals," she said. "The heart may be a lonely hunter but so is the soul." She egged me on to continue farther.

Stepping out of the sunshine was my beautiful creation Christina Mendez. "Tom, you made it!"

I took her into my arms and kissed both her cheeks. I then stood back and looked at her. She was as beautiful as I had envisioned her. Her large brown eyes, big sincere smile, and warm presence were enticing. Her husband, Jorge, was dead and she was now a widow and available. I was falling in love with my own character.

I put my arms around her waist and she did the same. Up the hill we walked. I breathed in her long brown hair and held her tightly, allowing the sun to drench me in its light.

Once we reached the top of the hill we were at my favorite place to be, an inviting deep-blue swimming pool. Bukowski waved to me from the other side. "I told you to stick with it," he said, knocking down a drink. Sitting next to him was my own creation, the tortured poet, Jared Gray. "To you," he said lifting his beer glass, beaming with joy under his dark sunglasses.

John Fante appeared in shorts and a Hawaiian shirt and put his arms around my shoulder. "Nice, hey kid? And I go nuts over these lovely Mexican ladies myself."

Blowing me away was seeing Sinatra and Dean Martin in their tailored light-blue and light-gray suits from the 1960s and straw fedoras, raising cocktail glasses. Ice cubes glittered in the sparkling sunshine. "Nice party, kid," Sinatra said. "Thanks for the invite."

"Come over here and throw your weight around, pally," Dean Martin told me.

Next thing I knew I was with Nelson Riddle's entire band singing his arrangement of "Fly Me to the Moon" while Sinatra and Dino sipped their cocktails. Molière and Camus appeared and sang along in French.

Beckett, Charlotte Brontë, Luigi Pirandello, Rainer Maria Rilke, Austin, Byron, Keats, Yeats, August Wilson, John Updike, Joyce, Graham Greene, Ellison, and dozens of writers I admired soon showed up poolside talking literature, art, life, and love. A young Marlon Brando, Vivian Leigh, Barbara Stanwyck, Bette Davis, Veronica Lake, and all the other movie stars and directors I ever admired and never got to meet joined the party.

"Happy?" my vibrant lady Christina asked.

"Happy," I answered.